Rosaline Labella Dumont

Three-Part Series
Part Two

MICHELLE WALTERS

Author's note

Part 2 of my Taken series, eventually out for all the fans to enjoy. It still amazes me how far I've come and to achieve such a goal, to be able to create a new world for someone else to live through my imagination.

I'm excited once again to share my stories with you.

I hope you've come to admire and love my characters through Taken Part 1 and continue with the three-part series that grows with passion, heartache, mysteries, and just plainly how someone copes through loss and change in the following chapters to come.

I would like to thank Beverly Harth for painting my cover, and just how I wanted it – I love it! You have an amazing talent. Thank you, Beverly. I would also like to thank my mother, Phyllis Webster, for all her love and support - my biggest fan. And most of all, to Richard Edwards from Beyond The Vale Publishing, for making all this possible.

Michelle

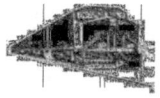

FOR MY NIECE

MELISSA WALTERS

You have a heart of gold and carry
it on your shoulders for all to see. I'm blessed beyond
measure to have a niece like you
in my life!
Love you always, my ladybug . . .

1

After being taken and cared for by the Vikings for over a year, Rosaline Labella Dumont was back in her homeland and living at the king's castle. When she first arrived, everyone was shocked and surprised to see her, especially King Louis, after hearing from his son, Philippe, that the Vikings took her. At first, they had no idea where to begin the search – then they were restricted with limited resources due to the measles epidemic when Rosaline disappeared. All they could do was hope and pray that she would persevere and somehow return to them. Nonetheless, now that she was back, Rosaline looked healthy and unscathed – much to the king's relief. Everyone greeted her with open arms and treated her with respect and concern, not knowing what she had been through.

In their uncertainty and curiosity to know the truth and facts about her disappearance and captors, they began to ask many questions, and she answered as best she could. Rose assured them that she was treated well and as a guest. The king was observing her while the small group asked their many questions. He was listening intently too, even though he was feeling optimistic with her return, yet, he could not help wonder, and noticed that even though she always smiled, Rosaline's smile never reached her eyes. *Why did she look so sad and not relieved or animated to be home amongst her own people?*

Not so long ago, Rose said her farewells to Olaf and Var – a family she came to trust with her life. Every waking moment she felt the pain of their loss; even though it was not a loss of death, it was much the same. She was separated from the only family she had come to love dearly – it still stabbed her at her heart – she needed her privacy to break down in tears.

Rose quickly explained the Viking's tragedy at sea while on a trading voyage, a voyage during which a few lives were lost, with most of the remaining crew severely injured. It was a tragedy that still haunts them, including her! Rose felt so lost that she could not yet explain her true feelings to anyone – she missed them terribly.

While caring for her during her amnesia recovery caused by her illness when she first woke up on their island, their care and humanity resulted in her adopting them spiritually and becoming a family. A family that welcomed and loved her for who she was; she grew close to the Viking clan. If it were up to her, she would have never left. After all, it was not her choice to leave; the Viking chief decided on her behalf that it was time that Rose returned to her own people.

Rose was exhausted and was growing weary of all the questions and opinions related to what she felt was more a private matter and all too soon to discuss in full detail.

After Rose explained enough to appease their basic curiosity about her life with the Vikings, she wished to be excused; she felt exhausted from the trip and wanted to retire before they queried her any further.

This was her first destination, and she saw no point in returning to her own home – a place that felt so far removed, especially with her parents no longer there, the people who made it her home – her home would never be the same without her parents around. The pain going there first was too much to bear; thus, Rose decided the castle was a better choice for now. However, right now, though, that peace and quiet would have been welcoming.

They listened to her last statement of the voyage incident and tried to understand; thus, they gave her time to mourn out of modesty.

In the beginning, Rose was constantly in her quarters. No one bothered her much and was grateful for the solitude. She mentally felt all her loss and loneliness in her seclusion and began to lose her appetite for food and life, and started losing weight. Rose could not see a future for herself, either here at the castle or her childhood home.

Prince Philippe, however, became worried and thought it was unhealthy to be cooped up all the time; Rosaline needed to get out and socialize. After giving her over a week's solitude and respecting her privacy, Philippe thought it best to visit Rosaline every day and personally invite her to join him for breakfast or the evening meal with walks in the garden. He said it might help her cope if she got out and mingled. On their outings and dinners, which he half forced her to participate in, he noticed she was despondent and did not socialize with anyone.

One evening, at the main dinner table, an event King Louis invited her to attend, Rosaline was lost in thought. As part of her nature with living with the Vikings for so long, out of habit, she picked up her duck meat with her hands and started biting into it, oblivious to the shocked stares she received. Upon taking her third bite, Rose looked up, noticed all eyes were on her and realized what she had done.

Half embarrassed, she just smiled politely, placed her duck back on her plate, picked up her knife and fork, and continued to eat the rest of the meal as was generally expected. While Rose started eating appropriately with her utensils, everyone went back to their normal conversation at the dinner table.

Rose's thoughts wandered once again to how she grew too accustomed to the Viking's eating habits. She felt awkward and uncomfortable at first, seeing how they consumed certain food with their hands. Eventually, she too started eating with her hands, mainly meat and bread. To her amazement, it was more satisfying that way - who would have guessed...

Life once again had changed; she was not sure if this was what she wanted, yet, she knew, for now, there was no other alternative.

Rose had to start all over with the old ways, an act she needed to uphold for her namesake and that of her parents. On the other hand, she could also not be bothered by what people might be thinking.

During her spell of extensive memory loss and being with the Vikings at that time, Rose forgot her most general memories and what her mother had taught her, lessons regarding life on how to be a proper lady in society. She learned new ways, experienced new things, and picked up other habits that no one would approve of when it came to a '*lady of the aristocracy.*' Rose no longer had the freedom to roam around and have fun – to feel free-spirited. As per their standards, she was expected to act as society expected, to be rooted in one spot, always acting polite and decent.

Not that she was not well-mannered with the Vikings; it came more naturally while being with them. And after remembering her parents were no longer alive, Rose always felt that she belonged with that Viking clan, especially when she had nothing to return home to. She felt more at home with the Vikings and her new family – a family she was separated from by circumstances beyond her control, forced to return to 'her own kind.' Now, many tears later, Rose felt cast out, as if she was being punished for something she could not comprehend.

Rose felt weird being at the castle without her parents around, occasionally having feelings of deja-vu, recalling snippets of her past. Lately, her mother and father were more frequently occupying her thoughts; she remembered and missed them more than ever before.

She wondered if news still got around and if Jessie would arrive soon and hoped that the reason for her delay was not ailing. Jessie was her guardian and was part of her family long before Rose was born and their town's healer. She desperately needed to see Jessie and wanted her company more than anyone else's. There was much she wanted to share with her.

Rose was so absorbed in her own world that the noise of chairs moving and loud speaking signified the meal ending, snapped her back to the present to her unwanted circumstances.

Life at the castle became more intense; the castle filled daily with new visitors, most curious about her return, and stories about her captives intrigued them. Daily guests wanted to ensure they were on the invitation list for the ball the king was organizing in Rosaline's honor to celebrate her safe return home.

Rose did not expect such a thing and was certainly not looking forward to it. At first, she informed the king that it was unnecessary for such a lavish event, especially in her honor – just to have returned home! He responded by explaining that her father was his most trusted and reliable friend, and he would have wanted this for her. Rose had the urge to argue the fact with the king, but she knew its futility; instead, she simply smiled and thanked him politely.

The days were almost all the same, starting with breakfast, followed by some fruitless activities in which Rose was forced to partake, then dinner with the king and his guests, after which she would always excuse herself and retire to her chambers for some solitude.

*M*ore than a month had passed since her arrival and only a week left before the ball, which she had much dread for. While with the Vikings, Rose would rise early for her daily chores; this morning, she became restless and bored with barely a reason to get up. Most of her days were spent in her chambers, seldom invited by someone or another to include her in their events, which was uneventful and not productive as the duties she was used to having with Popi - her adopted mother figure with the Vikings.

Not that she did not have fun there; their duties fitted in their lives, and she immersed herself into tasks and activities that had a purpose or a goal - and when it was time to relax or have their ritual celebrations, they went all out! She missed the continuous busy life.

Rose was in dire need of some fresh air and *alone!* She knew if she mentioned an outing, it would only result in more fussing over her, with the ever-so courteous Prince Philippe planning a picnic or some other outdoor activity to accommodate her.

She was not in the mood for the constant staring from the company that attended these outings, eyes watching her every move. Philippe was a dear, doing his utmost to make her feel welcome and at home, but it was becoming too much. His constant presence and wanting to please her was overwhelming; Rose needed to feel a little of the freedom she had lost and wondered if she'd ever feel better and accept her destiny, which was not so clear nowadays.

She needed space outside this room where she could feel comfortable to be herself; with this in mind, she needed a disguise. Rose still had her Viking clothes, made by Popi and her two daughters, which included two woolen cloaks with hoodies attached. The red one would be too noticeable, making the white one the obvious choice. Urged into action by her new adventure, she quickly dressed in her most common Viking outfit and put the white cloak on.

The sun was still rising when she covertly left her room and quietly sneaked out the servants' stairwell. When she entered the kitchen, the only way with a back door as far as she knew, a few servants noticed but let her be on her way. Rose was grateful that it wasn't so busy at this hour yet. When stepping outside, she covered her head with the hoody – feeling relieved that her escape plan went unnoticed with unwanted attention. She felt a little excited being so sly.

As Rose walked with no destination in mind, she thought of the whispers she overheard. Not everyone knew where she was or what happened to her, and she was not in the mood to explain to strangers about her 'abductors' – as they called them. The king and Philippe knew a little, and that should surely suffice, for now. They were also not sharing any information as she was told.

She understood that they were simply concerned, thinking the worst of the Vikings as they were regarded as common barbarians by society. Therefore, everyone felt sorry for her and assumed the worst. Rose knew she would have to explain the full extent of her story at some point, but not now; her heart was still aching to be with them.

Rose walked far out to the meadows where the cows were roaming – what she wouldn't give for a horse right now to fly across the field, not a person in sight. Every day on the Viking Island, she rode around freely, exploring the beauty and wonders the island offered.

She took a deep breath and relaxed for the first time since arriving. Rose was lost in thought and wondered what the Vikings were doing right now and tried to picture them all in her mind going about their odd jobs. It made her homesick. She realized that those days, that life on the island was over, and as far as she could see, unlikely to return. Popi gave selflessly, a loving and caring mother figure, the one who gave her so much to live for. Perhaps she should start accepting her life here and attempt to go on, accepting what each day had to offer, whatever came her way. For Popi's sake anyway, she had saved her life, and now it was time to live it.

Rose needed something to distract her mind from her sorrows, maybe start a hobby of some sort to keep her mind busy while she figured out the next step and perhaps also the next phase in her life.

While clarifying her troubled mind and thoughts and trying to come up with something worthwhile to keep her busy, Rose heard a yelling sound. It sounded like an animal was distraught. At first, she could not identify the direction of the noise but followed it as best she could. She walked between the cattle, who also started to moan with her invasion. There were cows everywhere making a noise, so she stood still and tried to hear the odd moan of a stress call. It was quiet for a few seconds, then it came again to her right, and she turned in that direction.

The ground was uneven due to digging and covering it up again to find a water flow, almost like finding a waterhole for a well. Not far was a small hole in the ground dug up long ago for drinking water for the animals. When Rose closed in towards the main waterhole, it was surrounded by a few cattle; disturbed by her presence, they all departed immediately, except one.

Rose then noticed the problem. It was a medium-sized circle and was big enough to climb in, but no one knew its depth, only the person who dug here who might be long dead.

Inside this drinking-hole was a calf trying to get out! Hanging on for dear life – calling for help to his helpless mother, who stood by watching and moaning as well. She was anxious for her child – not being able to help it. It was a sad scene.

Without thinking or hesitating, Rose threw off her cloak and shoes, grabbed the grass on the side, and climbed into the cold water. With this stranger in the water as well, the calf, seemingly with new hope, started splashing and fighting for its life. Rose used her legs and pushed the calf closer to the edge. When it had a grip, she used all her strength to heave the calf back on dry land. All exhausted, Rose gained her breath before climbing out herself.

The calf was shattered, trying and fighting for who knows how long to get out; it just sat there motionless. With satisfaction and wonder, Rose witnessed as the mother examined her child and gave a loud moo sound. Rose saw the interaction between them and was touched by their affection. She had never seen this among animals before and thought of how hopeless the mother must have felt by not being able to help her baby.

With such a simple task, Rose felt good inside and not so useless. She sat fixed on the same spot when climbing out, tears running down her cheeks with emotion. The calf started to stand with shaky legs, and after walking around a little, it came closer to Rose and sniffed. She did not move in case she scared the animal. It was almost as if it was saying thank you. She slowly lifted her hand, touched it on the side of the face, and said through teary eyes and smiles, "It's a pleasure!" The mother was curious as well, strolled over to join them, and was sniffing her head. Without knowing what to expect, the cow licked Rose full in the face. She burst out laughing and said, "Don't mention it – it was the least I could do to help!"

Rose shook her head, thinking she must be going insane speaking to cows. The animals walked off away from the water to feed further afield. She started shivering and stood up to ring her dress dry as best she could and put her shoes back on. She grabbed the cloak from the ground and wrapped it tight around her. Freezing, she slowly walked back to the castle. Rose was still on the castle grounds; hence, there was no danger of her being out alone, or so she thought.

Not far from the scene was a man enjoying the fresh air of the early morning. He, too, came out to the fields to be alone. He arrived just in time to witness the whole rescue ordeal and could not help but be amazed at this young woman for her bravery. She was wise to use her legs and not her arms. The calf would have pushed her down, trying to survive, not knowing any better. He would have intervened if that should have happened and so stayed rooted to his spot. He had never witnessed a scene like he had today, the emotion and affection she expressed – he was intrigued by this beautiful woman and had to meet her before she disappeared.

Rose was deep in thought – wondering whom to approach regarding the waterhole problem and unsure how it could be fixed. The king was no good; he would not bother himself with such petty things. Perhaps Philippe would help, but then again, no, not him. To share her concerns would highlight that she went out alone, unescorted, which might bother or worry him further. He was always kind toward her and constantly made light conversation at the dinner table. Rose was fond of him; he would make a good King one day.

The best alternative was to approach Prince Antoine, Philippe's younger brother, with the matter; as she recalled, he was easy to speak to. She felt more comfortable discussing this with him, especially with them being around the same age. After deciding that, she thought of a way to fix the hole – lost in thought...

"Excuse me, miss!" came a male voice behind her.

Rose jumped with fright and was startled nearly to death; she thought she was alone! Although it was too late to hide her face, she lifted the hood over her head and turned to face the stranger.

The man was tall, well-built, and not dressed as a commoner. She was astonished at how good-looking he was – and those eyes! They made her feel uneasy. It reminded her of someone.

"Do I know you?" Rose asked.

His smile made her more curious, stunning her; he was really dashing.

"No, my lass, I would have remembered if I ever met a damsel like you. I want to add that what I saw you perform in the waterhole was brave, and not many would have helped the poor creature."

She felt uncomfortable. He was staring with too much interest and walked closer toward her. It reminded Rose of her attacker on the Viking Island – fear took over. She took a step back and looked around to see if anyone was about, fearful that something should happen. He addressed her as if she were a common laborer and not a lady. Rose could not blame him for thinking that because she was dressed as one.

Suddenly realizing what he just said, if he saw the whole scene, why was he not the first to take action to help the creature? Rose reacted in anger, allowing rage to overcome her fear, and responded, not knowing he only came on the scene once she climbed in the shallow well.

"Instead of helping the creature, you simply looked on. I'm sure someone else would have helped, though not you, for you stood hiding and not caring for the cries of distress. And if I, a woman, did not take action, you would have allowed it to drown!" Rose tried to act brave, yet he still came closer. "I beg you, whoever you are, not to harm me, or you'll be sorry!"

He was amazed at her approach toward him. He had this overwhelming urge, an impulse that even surprised him, to enfold her in his arms and kiss her – for the life of him, he knew not why. It was never his intent to harm her, though he noticed the fear in those beautiful eyes. She must belong to

14

someone important in the castle. He would find out who she works for, even if it was the last thing he did. He put his hands up and took a step back.

"No need to call the cavalry. And to enlighten you, I arrived just when you entered into the water, I would have helped, but it seemed you had everything under control! I just thought of introducing myself. My name is Ollie Waters, and what may yours be?"

"I'm no concern of yours. Good day to you, sir," after which Rose turned around and hastily walked back to the castle.

While watching her half running away, he shouted, "Will be seeing you around then!"

Rose was upset by the whole incident, captivated by her own thoughts, '*the audacity of it all!*' When he shouted his last words, she almost tripped and went ice cold. She pulled the cloak tighter around her. His words brought back painful memories; those were nearly the same last words Thord told her before departing on his voyage – and her last kiss – Rose will never forget! – '*Look after yourself! I'll be seeing you soon.*' – before he turned and walked out of her life forever!

Tears were streaming down Rose's face as she ran through the kitchen again, up the servants' staircase to her room. The sun was long up; undoubtedly, many of the guests were wandering around, yet thankfully, she reached her quarters without anyone noticing. Her handmaiden, Clara, was busy tidying the room and jumped with fright at the lady's sudden entrance. Rose wiped her eyes dry and asked Clara to prepare a bath and bring something to eat. For some reason, she was starving.

When the food arrived, she ate while waiting for the tub to be filled. After which, she had a long relaxing bath, got dressed appropriately, and then went looking for Antoine.

The castle was abuzz, in full preparation for the upcoming ball. Dressmakers were ordered to help many guests to be decently prepared for the event, but Rose had not yet thought of such things. She would need to put up with one sooner or later. They were all surprised to see her up and about, especially Philippe, who approached her with a broad smile.

"Lady Rosaline, I'm so glad to see you. How are you feeling today? You are looking livelier today than usual."

Philippe noticed her cheeks were all flushed, and there was a spark in her eyes. He was feeling hopeful that she was over her ordeal and coming out of her shell - he always liked Rosaline. She was a beauty to behold. Like the young man that he was, his thoughts were inappropriate - he could not help himself. Rosaline would make a beautiful bride, and by the looks of it, she would satisfy him in bed too.

Still, he wondered if she was innocent, considering that Vikings usually don't assault women; they are taken as slaves or killed in a ritual, which he heard should be an honor to be offered to their gods. Yet one could not help but wonder what she had to endure; she does not speak much of her time with them and keeps to herself.

Even if she were not innocent anymore, he would not hold that against her. All in all, Philippe was still a gentleman and would uphold the marriage agreement between their parents. He wondered if Rosaline knew, but no matter, for now, he would be her friend for as long as she needed one.

"Good day, Philippe. I'm feeling much better; thank you for your concern. I was wondering if you knew where I could find your brother, Antoine? There is something I would like to discuss with him."

Philippe was a good-looking man; Rose couldn't help but notice how masculine he had become since last she saw him. To top it all, he had a warm, playful personality, all features different from his father's - a positive aspect, from her viewpoint. Philippe has had his fair share of hardship, such as losing three family members in the plague; a mother, an older brother, and a younger sister. Through it all, he still remained the pleasant, positive person she knew since childhood. He was more inclined towards his mother's kind nature, the caring queen that Rose could still remember.

Philippe answered, "Something important, perhaps I could help?"

Rose gave her most dazzling smile, "Nothing to concern you; it's not important. You have too much on your plate at the moment for such trivial things." She looked around at the people buzzing about and the hired staff impatiently waiting for his approval for one thing or another, all the while listening in on their conversation.

He turned to his group and spoke with authority, "I will be with you shortly. Go about your duties." He turned back to Rosaline and said, "You have all my attention. I can help you find my little brother and show you where his chambers are. It's too complicated to explain. Follow me, milady."

He presented her with a slight bow that made her giggle. It was a good feeling to be able to laugh and smile again. He offered his arm, which she accepted, hooking hers through his, they started walking away from all the activity.

When nearing Antoine's door, Philippe asked her to wait outside while he went in to see if his brother was presentable for company. It was Antoine's private chambers where he did all his work as well. His room was more extensive than most; it was a small flat in itself, except that it had no kitchen. His living area was the first thing you saw when walking in, and not far was his writing desk, which was close to his balcony. His bedroom was private with a closed-door - where the servants or any unwelcome intruders would not bother him while sleeping.

The scene when walking in was not what Philippe would have expected from his little brother. There were three surprising faces - one more shocked than the other.

"Oh, my!" Philippe turned around and was about to walk out, then decided to turn back again and said, "By all that is holy, Antoine, if this were father walking in right now and not me, you both would be dead on the spot!"

Philippe turned to face the door while the two men quickly put their clothes back on and went on speaking, "How long has this been going on – no, I don't want to know! What you do and whom you sleep with is your business. You are my brother, and I love you, but for the love of God, please do this activity at night or in your bedroom, not where anyone can walk into your chambers. Or are you looking to be caught and hanged by your own father?"

When they were decently dressed, Philippe turned to face them again. He was angry; he was upset and disgusted but tried his best not to show it. He never expected this in a million years. Antoine was a good-looking young man, and the girls were always around him seeking out his company.

It must have happened spontaneously for them to be in the middle of the room on the floor. It was certainly not planned when the bedroom would have been appropriate at this time of day – especially if you wanted to hide your affairs.

Antoine was embarrassed and said nothing; he had nothing to say about the incident – what could he say? He had no excuse either and would not lie to his brother – deep down, he felt a little relieved.

Philippe went on speaking in a stern voice and displayed no expression, "I'm here on behalf of Lady Rosaline; she is seeking you out to discuss a certain matter," he went on talking as if his brother asked why, "No, I don't know why, but thought I'd show her where you spend most of your days. She's waiting outside at the moment. Are you ready to see her – are you up for a visit? I can make an apology and bring her later."

Antoine found his voice for the first time and said, "Sure, let her in, and can we talk later?"

Philippe knew about what and did not expect an explanation. "If you really need to speak, but as I said, please be more careful and private with your affairs. I will leave Rosaline in your care; I have more pressing matters at hand to attend to." Philippe said nothing to his brothers' partner or greeted him – he was still fuming. He walked out and smiled at Rosaline.

"He can see you now. I'm sorry I took so long. There was something important I needed to discuss with him first. I will see you later."

Rose could see something was amiss and asked, "Are you OK?"

"Yes, could not be better, milady." He kissed her hand and left her to enter the room.

When she entered, she saw the tense look on Antoine's face and wondered what was discussed that upset the two brothers so?

Antoine put his worries aside for now and stood up to greet Rosaline. He was delighted to see her; he took both her hands and kissed her on each cheek, polite as always.

"Lady Rosaline, it's such a surprise to see you. We were all so worried about your health; I hope all things are fine with you?"

"Antoine! As always, it's a pleasure to see you, and please call me Rose."

"Rose it is then. How can I help you, Rose?" Smiling and offering her a seat.

"There is a matter I would like to discuss, and I was wondering if you would be able to help," Rose told him about her morning and the waterhole incident, leaving out the part with the stranger.

"Wow! That was brave of you! We have heard of this before; it's not the first time a calf falls in there. That one was lucky you were around. Still, I have no inkling how to fix that problem. Actually, no one seems to care, until now."

Rose was excited about this project and replied, "I have a suggestion if you'd listen to it?" It was also something to keep her mind busy.

"I'm all ears." Antoine returned her smile.

"Well." She was confident with her plan and explained, "What we can do is expand the area around the hole, so the water is shallow enough to walk in and drink. However, we first need to build a small fence around the central hole so nothing can get in. Then we can start digging around the area. So, the hole itself can still produce water around it without any drowning." She waited for an answer.

Antoine looked at his companion, who was still in the room, and they both smiled at the idea.

"It sounds reasonable! However, it will be muddy. Perhaps we could use stones to keep the sand in place and make it look more presentable. So, we dig around the central hole as you said and lay it with small stones - what do you think?"

"That sounds perfect! We just need loads of stones!"

"There should be a lot around the village area; we can use a horse and cart to collect them."

Rose was excited about her idea and smiled broadly and added, "And good diggers!"

"Excellent idea Rose, you are clever. I will get on it today so they can start immediately. Getting workers won't be a problem."

"Do you think I could perhaps be there to see the work done? I know I'm asking too much, but this is important to me." Rose was pleading with her eyes.

"I guess it's fine; you can't be there alone, though. This is Léo; he helps me with certain matters in my work. He can accompany you."

They both looked at Léo, and he smiled. "It would be my pleasure!"

"Oh, fantastic!"

2

*O*llie Waters was a loner and preferred it that way – he had his duties and always obeyed his prince, the future king. For now, they were comrades, brother in arms. He never interacted with the castle guests or their company; however, he heard the rumors about the girl that returned but has yet to meet her. Ollie was always sent on errands away from the castle. It was just by luck that he made it on time for the ball; he was not interested in socializing but was told to join by Philippe, so he had no choice and had to attend.

Ollie was standing with a group of people, not interested in their conversation, and just nodded from time to time; bored and uninterested in their chitchat, he graciously excused himself.

While he was getting a drink, he noticed a familiar face. He could not believe the redhead was at the event – was she a lady – then why was she dressed as a peasant in the fields the other day? He was sent away on business that same day and could not find out who she was. He returned yesterday and went to the fields, hoping to see her again. She was not there, but he noticed the hole had been changed; she must have had something to do with that.

She looked so uncomfortable standing by herself, wearing a light turquoise gown with her hair tied up to perfection – any painter's dream, posing for a portrait. Though he must be honest with himself, he preferred her hair hanging loose over her beautiful face when they first met in the fields. He had to speak to her again somehow.

Once again, Ollie was pulled into another group with a pointless conversation, where yet again, he had to graciously excuse himself when he spotted a close friend speaking to a few young ladies; he needed to have a word with his comrade.

"Evening, James." Ollie bowed to the ladies. "Evening, ladies, may I please steal my friend away from you beautiful ladies for a few minutes?" They all giggled, both men gave a slight bow before leaving, and the girls curtsied.

James half complained, "Smooth Ollie, why would you want to drag me away from those beautiful, innocent young girls? You should join me, not drag me away!" They both turned to look at the girls, who giggled once again.

"Thank you, but no, not my type, James."

"How do you know who's your type if you're not willing to try?"

"There is another that you can perhaps help me with? Since you are acquainted with almost every person here, you should know who she is."

"For you, I will try my best. Who and where is she?" James waited for him to point her out. He was happy to help Ollie for once to get a lady friend. Since the death of his wife, he has not been keen on other women.

"She's the only redhead at this ball!"

James didn't even bother to look. He knew exactly who the young lady was. He looked at his comrade; he was happy for a second that Ollie was showing interest in a woman again, but she was off-limits; he wouldn't even dare go there.

"Stay away from her," —straight to the point— "She's off-limits!"

"Why – who is she?"

"You have no idea, do you? That is Rosaline Labella Dumont, the one that went missing for over a year. Both her parents died of the plague, and then she was taken. No one knows where she was, and they are keeping that a secret. Rumors have it that she's to wed our future king, and may I add, your friend as well!"

Ollie was very much interested in her and decided he would speak to her anyway; no one else was. The poor girl looked lost and disinterested in the events around her.

"Thank you, James; you may go back to your groupies now."

James stopped him before he could walk away. "Please tell me you're not going over to speak to her?"

"Just to introduce myself – there's no harm in going over to greet her."

"Don't be daft, my friend! Leave her be; you are asking for trouble going over there. Don't tell me I did not warn you. I'm off... there are many pretty faces here to choose from instead."

Ollie was already walking away; he was not interested in the young and childish girls that James was always hanging around with, or any other woman for that matter. Not for a long time – until now! He felt compelled to greet her. If she was to wed the prince, then he will respect that. There's nothing wrong with building a friendship.

Rose was hiding, trying to avoid all the stares that came her way, and hiding from the men who desperately sought to dance – the place was full of gossip about her. She was standing close to a few older women sitting at the back. She already danced with two strangers and had four more names written on her card for future dances. Rose was thinking hard of a way to get out of the main hall. Perhaps a walk in the gardens would save her from all these people.

Ollie approached Rose from the side while she was deep in thought – once again.

"Evening Lady Dumont!" He smiled innocently.

Rose turned and was taken aback to see who greeted her. "You!"

He bowed and took her hand. "I thought I'd come over and apologize for the other day. It would seem I gave you a fright when approaching you in the fields." He kissed her hand and let it go.

Rose just stared like an idiot without saying a word, stunned to see him here of all places. He went on speaking, thinking she was ignoring him on purpose.

"In my defense, it was surely a misunderstanding, you were dressed like a peasant and not as a lady, and may I add you were all alone? If I'd known who you were, I would have offered to walk you through the castle doors." Wondering why she was dressed like that and alone in the first place.

Rose was irritated with the explanation of his actions. Finding her voice, at last, she spoke up, "So... me being a lady gets you to treat me kindly, but being a peasant girl gets to be treated unkindly! What kind of a man are you? All women, no matter their status, should be treated as equals."

She was disgusted with this man. His beautiful face and infectious smile would not work on her. Therefore, she attacked him further. Knowing a lady and a peasant women's status was different, *'but we were still women, and we all want the same thing – to be treated with respect from any man!'*

"So, you have the right to attack me, thinking I was a peasant, but being a lady gets me safely to my door. How is that fair? And if you believe that this was an apology on your part, then you are sorely mistaken and should try harder – or not at all!"

He could not take his eyes off her beauty and the way the dress complimented her blue eyes. "Excuse me, Lady Dumont, my plan was not to attack you that day or any other woman on any other day. It would seem you misjudged my behavior towards you. I was curious to meet the woman who jumped into a waterhole to save a calf from drowning."

Ollie was trying to persuade her. It was not in his nature to ill-treat any woman. There was something about her – he just wanted her in his arms – to hold her and kiss her until all her worries disappeared. As if their bodies were magnetized, forcing him closer toward her. He had to fight the urge not to get closer and stand at a respectable distance. Also, all eyes were on her as well, which meant on him too at the moment. He wondered if she was ever ill-treated at some point by the fury in her attack on him.

"Well, I am sorry if I offended you in any way, milady, and I do apologize to you for making you think ill of me. That was not my intention."

"I am sure! And I beg you to keep this to yourself, Sir..." She forgot his name and still did not trust him.

"Oh, so you have secrets – who are we keeping this from, and who helped you to fix the waterhole problem?"

"Wouldn't you like to know!" She was aloof towards him. Still worked up a little, Rose relaxed after that outburst, then asked, "So who are you anyway?"

He gave a bow. "I am Sir Waters – Ollie Waters – forever your servant, milady."

Just then, Philippe joined them. He gave a bow, kissed Rose on the cheek, and said, "Lady Rosaline, you look stunning tonight, definitely the most beautiful woman here. How is your evening so far?"

Rose curtsied. "Thank you, Philippe. You always flatter me; however, I do believe you are mistaken." She smiled innocently.

"Believe what you may, milady. Ah, I see you met my dear friend, Sir Waters." Philippe liked Ollie; he was a decent man. The respect went both ways. Ollie would do anything to please him and was looking forward to be working with the future King of France.

"Evening Philippe, I came over to introduce myself to Lady Dumont; however, I believe I've made an awful impression on my own behalf." They bowed together in greeting.

Philippe answered, "That can't be true, Rosaline. What has this man said to you?" Smiling playfully – clueless about their previous exchanges.

"Prince Philippe, we were just getting acquainted." Rose informed him before 'that man' said anymore. She would like to keep her personal outings private.

"Please let me do the honors of introduction. Rosaline, this is Sir Ollie Waters, a close friend, and when I'm king, he will join me and become my captain in arms. I have come to trust his judgment. He is a good man."

Ollie gave a nod of thanks and gave a slight bow to Rose.

"Ollie, this is Rosaline Labella Dumont, my dear friend since wee ages. Our fathers were close friends. Her father was the head of our cavalry and won many battles. One brave man and respected by many and missed dearly."

Rose thanked him for his kind words and curtsied to them both.

"Now that the introduction is done, may I ask for this dance, milady?" Philippe held his hand out for her to take, and she accepted, "Please excuse us, Ollie," Philippe said before leading Rose to the dance floor.

Rose noticed Ollie was waiting for her, most probably to continue their conversation before the prince interrupted them. She agreed to dance with a few other men to avoid another confrontation and hoped he got the message.

*O*llie did not know why this woman had an effect on him. He, of all people, was more confused about his feelings. He felt attracted to her in a weird sense that excited and scared him.

Ollie was an honest man, true to himself and his heart. Loyal to his most trusted friends. Since he lost his wife, who was pregnant with their child, he joined the army when the prince came looking for willing comrades and threw himself into his duties. Since then, he had no time for himself or any flirtations with women. He was thankful for the distraction and gave all he had to the regiment. He became the second general in command, close to Prince Philippe.

Ollie decided to refresh his drink. While waiting for his order, he looked around at all the people laughing and enjoying themselves. The place was humid and too crowded to his liking. He needed some fresh air and decided a walk in the gardens would do the trick and try to clear his mind.

It was a lovely evening outside, and many couples were doing the same, having private conversations. He passed one he knew – James. He was engaged with a young filly, definitely taking advantage of her. Ollie just shook his head and was thankful he was unseen. Hoping not to interrupt another couple in inappropriate activities in the gardens, he decided to walk further to the outskirts of the garden to be alone with his thoughts.

While failing hopelessly in the efforts to clear his head of the lovely Lady Dumont, Ollie heard a noise behind a hedge close by. He walked over and noticed someone was hiding. He took it upon himself to inspect and handle the situation without involving anyone, and in so, avoiding a big scene. He would throw the person out himself without a big commotion – hopefully, this person will comply.

Ollie walked towards the hedge and spoke up, "Excuse me, sir; do you have an invitation to be attending the ball?" Thinking it best to be polite at first, a person never knew if he was hostile. The person moved further into their hiding place, probably hoping he was speaking to someone else or hoped not to be found.

"Sir, please, I don't want any trouble! I see you hiding there – please come out and confront me, or you leave me no choice but to use force. I don't want to make a scene, but I will have

31

no control over the matter if you do not face me this instant!"
Getting angry and expecting the worst.

To his surprise, it was a local woman, and she looked scared.

"Ma'am, why are you hiding – what are you doing here?"
Ollie relaxed again, knowing he could handle this on his own.

The woman was still half hiding and spoke for the first time,
"Sorry, milord, I've come looking for a particular person. I'm
not here to cause any trouble, milord. I was hoping that
perhaps this person would be walking in the gardens so I can
speak to them." Not wanting to give any information out to
whom. She did not know who to trust.

"Who is this person you planned to meet? Perhaps I can
help you find him; then you can be on your way." Thinking it's
one of the men inside that was her lover. She was not an ugly
woman. Most of the established men often like to bed a peasant
woman.

"It's not planned, milord; this person does not know I'm
here seeking them out." She thought he looked like an honest,
decent person, or else she would be long on her fanny on the
ground outside by now and not talking to her. Therefore, she
went on speaking, "I have not seen her in a long time and was
hoping to see her tonight."

She? So, it was a woman. "Why have you not sought her out
in a different way by a letter or invitation? Why hide here in
the bushes?" Ollie was mystified with her ways of seeking a
person out. Perhaps she wants revenge on her lover's wife. Still,

he was interested in who this person was. He was bored and needed a little distraction away from his thoughts.

"Who is this woman? Maybe I can call on her to meet you, but in my presence, of course."

Jessie thought hard on the matter and urgently needed to see Rose. She went through a lot to be hiding here and waiting. She truly wanted to trust him, needed to trust him. She had to know if it really was Rose and that she was OK. Any other way was difficult. Jessie did not want to be noticed or involve the king or prince. Rose was guarded like a hawk, or so she heard, and every visitor went through many channels. This was her only way. She was unsure if Rose would ever take a walk outside this evening and decided to trust him. He was her only hope now.

Ollie waited patiently for her to speak again.

"Her name is Rosaline Dumont, milord."

"Lady Dumont?" He was surprised and did not expect her name to be mentioned. "How do you know her, and what do you want with her?" He felt protective over the lady and was worried whether this woman had ill feelings towards her for some reason.

"Please, milord, it's personal. I don't want anyone knowing I'm here. Can you help me?" Trusting him to keep the secret, she hoped he would.

"I'm not sure I can help with that one." Trying to protect Rosaline, not sure what all this means. She went through a lot recently – so he heard – and he wanted to keep her safe.

33

Jessie noticed his facial expression change when she mentioned Rose's name. Did he like her – was he trying to protect her? In that case, this might just work. She tried a different approach.

"I don't mean any harm to her person, milord. You can tell her in private that Jessie is seeking her out and is waiting for her. So, it can be her choice to come."

Ollie was even more intrigued by Rosaline and her secrets.

"I will see what I can do. However, I promise nothing."

Jessie was grateful. "Thank you, milord! That is all I ask."

Once inside, Ollie started searching for Rosaline. She was dancing with the prince again. He caught her attention for a few seconds and signaled for her to meet him outside. He looked serious and was hoping she would comply.

Rose was wondering what his intentions were this time. After the dance, she excused herself, walked outside, and stood on the opposite side of the terrace. The night air was delightfully cool after all the dancing. She noticed Ollie waiting for her and ignored him by looking up at the sky, enjoying the cool fresh air. She closed her eyes for a few seconds then suddenly heard him speaking next to her – she jumped with fright.

"So, you ignoring me, are you?" He smiled playfully at her and was amused by her actions.

"I am doing no such thing! I am trying to enjoy the cool air and to be alone for a while." She looked straight at him, hoping he would take the hint and leave. Rose was not in the mood to continue their unfulfilled conversation from earlier.

"Well, you might be pleased to know that I have been sent for you!"

"Oh... and who would send you to seek me out, Sir Waters?" She suspected he was joking and trying to tease her.

"She said it was personal and to tell you in person and privately. No one may know she is here. I was confused at first, but I find it very interesting that it's you she's seeking out?"

"If you are looking for a way to interest me in walking with you alone in the gardens, then you are sorely mistaken!" Rose started to walk away.

"She gave a name that might be of interest."

Rose stopped and turned about and waited for him to go on.

He looked at her to see her expression when he mentioned the woman in waiting.

"She told me to inform you that her name is Jessie, and she is waiting in the gardens for you."

Rose was almost in tears when she heard her name. "Where is she? Take me to her at once!" She was instantly off in her own direction. Ollie had to stop her and led her in the opposite direction. When they eventually stopped, she anxiously looked at him questionably; he said to call her name.

"Jessie?" Rose called out.

Jessie came out of her hiding place, "Rose, my dear, dear Rose - it is you!" They both ran to each other, hugging and crying in each other's arms. "I thought I lost you forever, but always hoped you'd return. I looked everywhere for you and waited a long time before I went to my own home again."

It broke Jessie when she had no other choice but to give up searching.

Rose was crying so hard she could not speak and just held onto Jessie.

Ollie could see this was personal and felt a little uncomfortable with all the crying. He was not sure what to do or say, thus offered to keep watch that no one came and stepped aside so they could have their privacy. He could still hear what they were saying, though.

Jessie went on to say, "You look well. That was all I ever hoped for you. I just had to see for myself that it was truly you that everyone was speaking about," Jessie touched Rose's hair lovingly and said, "And look at your hair, back to the way it's supposed to be. I always told your mother she was paranoid by coloring your hair."

Rose's tears subsided after a while. "Oh, Jessie, how much I've missed you and wished you were in good health. I have so much to tell you and nothing bad, my dear friend, but why have you not come to the castle sooner? Why are you hiding in the gardens?"

Ollie thought, '*I asked the same question and got no answer.*' He waited to hear her explanation.

"I will tell you later in private. It's a long story, my child." Jessie hugged her again. "I'm just so happy you are back! I must be off soon again, and you can't go missing from the ball for too long." Jessie consoled.

"No! Please stay, Jessie? I missed you so and thought the worst when I heard nothing of you when I returned. I'm so thrilled you are alive and well." Rose held on to her once again.

"There, there, my dove." A name Rose's parents used to call her, which brought fresh tears to her eyes.

They spoke for a while before Ollie interrupted them, "Excuse me, ladies. Not to be rude, but it's going to look weird that we were seen walking together in the gardens and went missing for a while." He could see Rose did not want to leave this woman so soon after their meeting again. However, there will be questions, and he was not sure what to say if they wanted this private?

"He's right, Rose. We will meet again sometime. There will always be a way to meet again."

"No! I have so much to tell you now, and you have as well with hiding here to seek me out and the hair explanation too!" Rose was adamant about not leaving Jessie again after their reunion.

Ollie thought hard about this dilemma. Rosaline, not wanting to leave, made it hard to keep this a secret, which the other woman was trying so hard to uphold.

"OK, I have a plan. You go back to the ball and dance, have a drink or two, then excuse yourself for being tired and that this was a little too much too soon. Whatever story works for you – I believe the prince will believe anything you say. Then I

37

shall take your lady friend to the kitchens' side entrance and lead her to your chambers. Thus, you can have all the time to share stories to your heart's content. How does that sound?"

Rose could not believe that she did not think of that sooner. "Sir Ollie, that's perfect!" She looked hopeful at her friend and asked, "Will you do this Jessie? Will you wait for me in my room?"

"I guess I can. We will concern ourselves later about when I have to leave again. Perhaps you can help with that again, kind Sir?" Jessie looked at the handsome man with assurance; she knew he fancied her Rose.

"If I'm present at the time and not sent on errands, I will see what I can do. For now, you will have to wait in hiding once again. If it's not an inconvenience, would you mind waiting at the kitchen entrance? It will be better than waiting here. I shall try not to be long."

When walking off together, Rose thanked him again.

"Thank you, Sir Waters. I do appreciate your concern and thoughtfulness. I am ever so grateful for your discretion on my behalf."

Ollie gave her a nod and smiled. "This is all so alien to me. I have no idea what is going on. All I know is that you are old friends with the woman and that you have not seen each other in a long time and missed each other dearly."

They walked at a respectable distance from each other while in conversation. As a man should, he respected the woman and knew she was spoken for, and marrying the prince means she would be queen one day. He must really try to get her out of his mind! Some couples saw them walk together, so he was obligated to walk her back to the entrance before returning to Jessie.

"My story is very complicated, Sir Waters. Perhaps I shall share some details at a later date. I guess I owe you that much for helping me with this."

When they reached the entrance of the ball, Ollie gave a low bow, then said goodnight, knowing he won't see her soon. She curtsied and bid him a good night.

She was about to enter when he called out, "Oh, Lady Rosaline, I have no idea which rooms are yours?" He almost forgot to ask.

Rose smiled. "On the second floor, the first door on the right. Please tell Jessie I will try to be quick." They parted, each in their own direction.

When passing James's spot once again, a girl came out blushing, fixed her garments and hair, and rushed past Ollie. James came out not long afterward and called on his friend. James was a loose cannon, and Ollie was glad he had not seen Rosaline with him.

"Ollie, my friend, come to I. Where's your partner?"

"What do you mean?" He was worried that James had seen Rosaline and did not want an earful of how wrong that was.

James laughed, "Don't say you left her in the bushes?"

In a sense, he was right. Jessie was waiting in the bushes for him, hopefully close to the kitchen entrance this time. He was irritated with James and his manners by how he treated women.

Ollie said, "Let's get one thing straight, my friend; I am not that kind of man to do inappropriate things outside in the gardens as you do! I am on my own and enjoying the cool evening breeze."

"You are so hopeless when it comes to women, Ollie. I should give you a few pointers on the matter." James was smiling and pleased with his earlier achievements.

"Thank you for your concern, but I am just fine the way I am."

"Where are you off to now – are you not going back inside to mingle? I hope you put those notions of Lady Dumont out of your mind?"

"All gone, James, not to worry. It was just a little interest in her mysteries." Ollie started walking away to show that the conversation was over and said, "I'm suddenly starving; if you will please excuse me, I think the kitchen has a plate waiting for me..."

James shouted after him, "Will be seeing you around then when your belly is full," and turned laughing toward the party. He could not understand why Ollie could not get over his dead wife and take another or just bed a few at least. His thoughts of Ollie instantly disappeared when he saw more young girls ahead.

When Ollie arrived at the kitchen, he called for Jessie, and she came out of hiding. He was wondering why she was so scared to be caught.

While they took the servant's stairs, Jessie wondered about this man and why he was so eager to help.

"Are you not worried that someone might see you with me?"

Ollie laughed, "Not as worried as you would be! No, to be honest, the men don't judge, and the servants speak among themselves, so we are both safe on that matter."

"Do you do this often then, milord?" Wondering what kind of man he was and if he were suitable for her Rose. However, Philippe would disapprove of this man's feelings for his future bride.

They reached the second floor, and he took her to the first door on the right and answered, "What – sneaking strange women in rooms at night?" he laughed again, "No, ma'am, I'm not that kind of man, and I'm still trying to get over a loss myself. It's hard to do when I'm always so busy." Ollie had no idea why he opened up on his personal life, but it was said. At a loss for words, he just smiled at her.

"Sorry for your loss. I guess we all lost someone through the epidemic."

He opened the door and stood aside for Jessie to enter. They both looked around the room and said nothing further. Rose's room had a spacious lounge, including a small balcony. Her sleeping quarters were private, with a curtain surrounding her bedroom area. Her bathtub was still there, full of water. Jessie

41

so wanted to climb in. After her long ride to get here and then hiding behind hedges and bushes – jumping over them all just to get in – she felt dirty.

Feeling a little uneasy, Ollie decided to depart. This time he could leave the proper way down the main stairwell.

"Well, Jessie, it was lovely meeting you, and I wish you a pleasant evening further – until we meet again." He gave a slight bow and opened the door to leave.

It took Rose a little longer to get away than she thought. When she entered the hall, she resumed dancing and mingling as planned, had a few drinks, danced with Philippe once again, and later asked if she could be excused. Philippe thought nothing of it and bid her a good night.

3

*J*essie liked this strange, handsome man and wondered why Rose was so cold toward him. She felt the water in the tub; it wasn't that cold and still looked clean. She decided to have a bath before Rose showed up.

After feeling clean and fresh, she went to Rose's bed to wait there in case someone came in and found her. There was no explaining this to anyone. She felt safer hiding behind the curtains, which closed a vast space for the bedroom area.

When Rose came in much later, she found Jessie asleep on her bed. She went quietly to the kitchen to get a bottle of wine for them to share and a few snacks, knowing that this was going to be a late evening for them both.

After placing the food and drinks on her small dining table, she dressed in something more comfortable and joined Jessie on the bed, who woke up startled, forgetting where she was for a second.

"Oh dear, I'm so sorry for falling asleep on your bed! The anxiety of the day was too much for me, and the ride was long and hard too."

"Don't be silly, Jessie. I'm happy you agreed to stay with me, and you must please stay for a while. They don't bother me in my room when I decide to stay in, so you're safe from whatever you're hiding from. I've been so lonely these past few weeks since arriving back. I feel I don't belong here anymore! I would like to go home or just see it again; however, I heard it was given to another."

Rose stood to pour them each a glass of wine and placed the snacks in front of them on the bed while Jessie answered, "It will be good for you to see your home again. How are you really? Were you treated well where you were? I know the Vikings took you, and it broke me that I could not follow or knew where to go even if I had the means of transport." Jessie looked worried. "I promised your father I would take care of you, and I lost you soon afterward. You can't imagine what was going through my head at the time. I was dreadfully worried and felt so hopeless."

"I'm so sorry, Jessie! I promise you; I was in safe hands. I was treated with kindness and so much love from those people, and I miss them all terribly! Is it silly to say I want to go back?"

"I guess not, my dove. I'm happy they came to love you and accepted you, though I'm not surprised, just relieved by the news. So, tell me everything that happened."

Rose started from the beginning, from her days on the beach with Popi. Jessie asked many questions in-between to understand some of it. She liked this woman called Popi and hoped they'd meet someday. Jessie would like to thank her personally. It would seem they have much in common.

They finished the bottle of wine and snacks and spoke until the early hours of the morning. Jessie was extremely fascinated with her stories and these people and wanted to hear more. However, it was getting late, and they could hear some of the guests returning to their rooms. She decided to stop Rose so they could get some sleep and continue her story again soon. It was not what she had thought the Vikings would be like, or maybe just certain tribes were different like hers were; you had good, civilized Indians and those that attacked their own and preferred violence. Her tribe was attentive. They just wanted to survive and to be left in peace.

Much later that day, Rose heard movement in her room. Jessie was still sleeping, so she went to see who it was and found her handmaiden, Clara.

"Good day, Miss Rosaline. Sorry to have woken you. They told me to refresh your bath if you desire so?"

"That would be kind, Clara, and would you mind bringing food. Make it double and a pot of tea, please."

Clara wanted to do her duties first and walked towards the bed to pull the curtains open that surrounded it and asked, "Should I make your bed while you dress?"

Rose stopped her. "No, that will be all, thank you. I will be staying in today."

Clara found it weird how the lady jumped in front of her. She smiled inwardly, thinking the lady was hiding a lover. "Yes, miss, right away. They will be serving lunch soon. Would you not prefer to go down and eat?"

"No, not today. Please bring it up, and don't forget to double the amount." When Clara left, Rose pulled the bed curtain open and found Jessie awake and making the bed.

Jessie smiled, "Good morning, Rose. I have not slept like that in a long time. I slept like a baby!"

"Morning, Jessie." Laughing at the guilt Jessie was feeling of being so unperturbed.

"We still have much catching up to do. There will be a fresh bath soon, then perhaps we can take a walk later? I have clean clothes for you if you care to change. You must see the clothes they made me!" Rose went straight to her cupboard and also showed the last dress Popi made for her at the previous festival she attended.

Jessie was impressed and picked one that would suit her, and Rose got one out for herself. She felt so alive again with Jessie being with her.

Jessie noticed what Rose was planning to wear and voiced her concern, "Rose, you can't be wearing that out in the open! You should wear a lady's garment when attending a walk in the gardens. People will see you, and your mother would have disapproved!"

Rose laughed, "Yes, she would, but it's OK! I always wear them when I go out, so no one recognizes me. It is good to be alone sometimes without a full party. I feel so locked up even when I'm all dressed up and out, doing things with other people. It's not me, and I feel it will never be me again. I was always a free spirit. The life I had on that island was the kind of life which I want to live, not this one!"

"I know, dear. You were always your own person. Please don't forget that it's different here, and you will have to accept the change again. Your mother knew that as well – why do you think she was always so strict with you? I'm sorry if this upsets you, but it's the truth."

"I know, Jessie. One day at a time, for me, please accept this new me, and let's enjoy the day together."

Jessie laughed and poked her on the nose, "There is no new you – you've always been like this. I guess that place opened you up to be yourself. This is a good thing, and I'm glad you experienced that freedom and found your true self. I'm worried if you should get caught and all the questions you'd have to answer, which you are not ready to explain. They might just think those people brainwashed you. No women in the high-class would understand why you would want to go out dressed up as a common peasant person."

"That's true; I promise I will try to stop. It just feels good to be on my own. I guess I have many things to sort out in my mind; being with people blocks my thoughts, and I sometimes feel that I can't breathe."

"You're homesick, and I don't mean your birth home. You grew up and found a higher purpose in life and a place where you belong. I do understand. You were doing something good there with them, healing and learning the trade. The life there sounds so much like mine, as we Indians do. I'm proud of you and the strength you had to survive. You will survive this too, and I believe your parents would be proud!"

"Thank you, Jessie. That means a lot to me!"

When the meal arrived, they ate, then had a bath, and got ready for the day. It was midday; the lunch was over downstairs, and the other guests were relaxing in the parlors. The kitchen was cleaned with the lunch dishes, and only a few servants were left to start supper. Thus, it was easier for them to sneak out of the kitchen.

Rose took her to the waterhole to show her what she accomplished so far. She explained what she had to do to save the little one and that Antoine helped with her idea. The animals looked happier, feeling safe to walk in and drink the water. They built a fence around the hole so no innocent can fall in and drown, then expanded the hole further so the water could spread out more.

The two picked a shady spot to sit on the grass and enjoyed the quietness. They had a beautiful view of the cattle that were roaming around. Rose continued with her story where she left off, explaining all the Viking's rituals and beliefs, then went on where the English blindly attacked Cnut and the others. She had tears remembering it all again and the loss of Thord. They also had many laughs in-between.

Rose's throat was parched from all the talking and could have kicked herself for not bringing a picnic basket. She promised to continue with her story later; she wanted to give Jessie a turn to speak.

"Now it's your turn to share some! First, I remember you said something about my hair? You said my mother was paranoid - why? And why are you so afraid to be caught in the castle?"

"It's not that I'm afraid to be caught, but what might come out if I'm seen." Jessie looked stressed.

"What do you mean, Jessie? What may come out?"

"Remember I told you my mother came here many years ago to teach your kind what she knew about herbs. She wanted to help and share her knowledge and more. She also wanted to see and experience new things. Well, she did for a while. She lived close to the castle and helped the people around here and sometimes in the castle as well. Everyone respected her, but at the same time, they feared her for being different. She was treated well until everything changed." Jessie paused, wondering if she should go on or not.

Rose saw she was hesitant to continue and said, "I remember you saying something like that and also that she didn't stay for long, except you never explained why. If everything was going well, why did she leave?" Rose was curious to understand her friends' pain and willed her to go on.

Keeping something inside is not healthy, and maybe letting it go or sharing it will heal itself.

"Well, Rose. Why my mother left so abruptly was because she was sexually abused."

"Oh my, Jessie, I'm so sorry to hear that!" She wasn't sure what to say next and was not expecting such a ghastly tale.

Jessie continued, "At first, she was in shock and too scared to go home, but they all supported her, and that made her strong again. Later she found out she was pregnant."

"What – what did she do?"

"She decided to keep the child because it was a part of her too. She said it was not the child's fault the way it was conceived. She loved and protected that child with all her heart."

"So, you have a sister or a brother – where is the child now?"

"No, Rose, no siblings, only me." Jessie looked straight at Rose when she said that.

"Oh, Jessie!" Rose leaned over and hugged her friend. "I'm so sorry!"

She smiled at Rose. "I'm fine with it now. My mother loved me and showed me every day that I was meant to be in her life. She is a brave woman with a huge heart. She kept telling me that I was 'her' child and that I was born into love and acceptance. I wish you could meet her!"

"She does sound brave. I would love to meet her, hopefully, one day. Do you know who your father is then? Is that the reason why you don't want to be seen around the castle?" Rose just realized what she said. "Oh my, Jessie, it's someone of importance in the castle – who is it?"

"I can't tell you outright; I want to explain the way my mother explained it to me so you can understand more."

"OK." Rose waited for her to continue.

"Well, as I said, my mother had performed many healing favors in the castle, which brought her close to important people. Everyone knew her and what she could do. She helped Philippe's father; he was the same age as Philippe is now and not yet a king. My mother helped Prince Louis with his injuries and other illnesses that were to be kept secret. He was not a well-behaved man, and his needs were never satisfied.

"He was kind to my mother and trusted her with his many secrets; in doing so, he beckoned her a lot, also for his concubines that needed a quick fix for unwanted or unplanned pregnancies. My mom helped him and kept all his secrets until one day, everything went wrong. One of his floozies gave him a terrible disease, and his father found out. They had a fallout about his choice of women and his obscene lifestyle. His father, the king, forced some changes in his life, which Louis was not happy with.

"Not long after this happened, his father forced marriage on the future king, saying that a settled woman might ground him and make him grow up. Louis changed into an angry and pompous person around the castle. No one liked to be around him that much anymore.

"My mother was picking herbs in the fields one day to make extra potions for her short trip further afield. She used to ride out and give to the poor as well, who could not afford such luxuries. She liked to help as many as she could. My mother was paid for her duties in the castle; thus, she could afford to sleep in inns and support herself. Herbs grew all over in the fields, free to pick at leisure when needed. The people were very grateful for her help and concern.

"Those days, it was mostly kids that fell ill. My mother said that their systems were not used to all the germs that were going around. The adults were different. Their systems came to accept the germs – though not all. Anyways, on the same day, she was picking and looking for specific herbs and roots. The future king was out hunting with a group of men. They were all resting close to the river when she heard Louis calling her. My mother was washing her hands.

"Oh, on another subject and something to remember, which she told me as well - was never to wash what you pick straight away. Keep the soil on until you decide what to make, ointment, or medicine. Only then do you rinse it very well." She smiled at Rose, knowing she would want to know that, "My mother said the same thing to me when she was telling this story. It keeps the herb fresh and moist and won't dry out too soon, especially if you want fresh herbs and not dried ones. Anyway, she was very trusting toward others and went over to see Prince Louis to hear what he wanted; she was told that one of the hunters was injured. She took out an ointment for his arm and covered it.

"Louis was always friendly toward her in the past. When she got up to leave, the prince and another man offered to walk with her. She saw an exchange between the two and felt uneasy. My mother told him that she had to be on her way and was in a hurry. That's when it all happened.

"The other man hit her, and when she fell, he held her down while the prince mounted her. My mother said it happened so fast that she had no way of knowing it was coming or had time to react. She fought at first; however, it didn't help her situation. They got rough with her and she gave up fighting, knowing she would lose, so she just let it happen and prayed that it ended soon. Thankfully, it was only Louis; his companion was not bothered for seconds. They laughed when he finished and left her there as she was on the ground.

"She had all her small belongings with her already, as she always does on her trips inland. That was the day she left and went back to her own people and never returned. No one would believe my mother's story if she came out with it or even if they did; they would have done nothing in any case."

Rose was in shock and had no words to reply to such a story. She was thinking of her time on the Viking Island with her attacker and was grateful for Cnut's brave rescue. What do you say to another person who went through all that and survived the assault her mother went through? Rose could not imagine the pain and felt sorry for this kind woman who brought Jessie up - accepting her fate and the child she carried. Her mother was brave, courageous. A person could not imagine what she went through unless you went through that experience yourself.

"So now you know why I can't face him at the castle. Or want to be noticed by anyone, and I trust you will not tell this to anyone, my Rose. This is my secret that I trust you with now."

Rose noticed for the first time the resemblance she had with the king. She felt so much anger toward him, which was unlike her to feel toward another person. Even the one she killed, she did not dislike as much as the king right now.

"Your secret is safe with me, my dear Jessie. I can't understand why you never told my mother about this. She would have understood, and you would have felt lighter a long time ago. We were - are your family. I can't imagine what you must be thinking or going through right now, knowing your father is close by, a man that cruelly dishonored your mother!"

Jessie explained, "Your parents were the best thing that ever happened to me when arriving here for the first time. They accepted me as I am and included me as part of the family, which made me feel special and made me believe there are good people in this world. Telling them, they would have looked at me differently, and I did not want that. Also, your father was in regular contact with the king, and they were friends, so to say, I did not want to cause a rift between them.

"It was my burden, and I thought coming here to face my father might be easy. I was petrified and decided never to face that demon and just live my life as it was. I was happy until the evil came and destroyed everything and took you away from me too. I still blame myself. However, I've come to believe that everything happens for a reason; call it fate. You were happy there, and you will be again someday soon. You had to be taken once again – and come back again – perhaps at the end journey, it will be your choice where you want to be or where you feel at home."

"I'm confused? Taken again – what do you mean *again?*"

"Oh dear, yes, I will tell you everything you need to know, but right now, it's getting dark, and we need to get back inside."

Rose was so captivated by the story that she looked around and noticed it was getting dark for the first time – they stood up and sneaked back into her room. Luck was on their side, that once again, no one noticed. On the way up, Rose grabbed two bottles of wine and some bread and cheese. When they were safely in her room, Jessie forced her to dress for supper just to show face that no one seems suspicious of her disappearance.

"I can't leave you here by yourself!"

"Yes, you can, and you will. You can bring food with you, and while you're gone, I will eat the bread you grabbed and maybe sleep for a while. All this talking has made me tired. I will help you dress and look presentable, and you can be on your way."

Rose was not happy with this but complied with her dear friend.

*P*hilippe was glad to see Rosaline join his guests and was instantly by her side all the time. The king saw this and was worried about his son's feelings for her. She was an attractive young woman, and there was an agreement about their betrothal in the past. However, that changed since his eldest son's death, and now Philippe was heir to the throne. Rosaline was just a lady. His son had to marry a princess now, and him being so busy, he completely forgot to mention this to Philippe. He thought Philippe knew, which would have saved him from explaining it to his son. He let them have tonight, but this infatuation with the girl had to stop.

Even if the marriage was still on, the king felt that Rosaline was not suitable anymore. She wasn't the same person when her parents were alive. Her manners and actions as a lady should be and act had changed.

Rose wished the meal would end soon so she could excuse herself. People frequently surrounded her, and Philippe was in regular conversation with her too. Not that she was more relaxed now and enjoying herself. There were things she wanted to know from Jessie, and the curiosity was eating at her. After the meal, drinks and tea were served. While the people were helping themselves, Rose thought about how she could excuse herself or even sneak away.

Antoine was watching Rose for a while and decided to approach her. "Evening Rose, you look preoccupied – is everything alright?"

"Antoine! Yes, thank you." She always felt she could be open and trust him with anything. "Actually," she chuckled, "I want to leave, but I feel if I excused myself as I often do, people would think I'm rude or whatever story they can think of. Sneaking off seems like a better option. Yet, I appear to be so noticeable tonight. I may just as well stand on a table or a chair, the way people are staring."

He laughed at her expression of annoyance. "Rose, if you want to leave, just leave! Bugger the people here and do what you feel is right or do what you want to do. It's not an obligation to stay until the last person leaves. Come, I'll walk you out, then perhaps you will feel better." Rose took his offered arm, and he led her out to the entrance hall.

He smiled kindly at her and said, "There, now go about your way."

"Thank you, Antoine. Please tell Philippe I... um..." She was always excusing herself that for the first time, she actually felt guilty doing it so often.

"It's fine, Rose. I will tell him you overate and are feeling the after-effects – if that is alright with you?"

"That is fine. Thank you once again, Antoine. Good night and enjoy your evening further." He bowed, and she curtsied.

Antoine was about to turn to return to the guests when he noticed her direction was to the kitchen and not the stairwell. He wondered why; thus, he decided to wait to see what happens next. It intrigued him more when she never returned to take the main stairwell. He was confused why Rose would take the servant's steps to her room. Antoine would call on her tomorrow to find out what she was hiding and warn her to be more careful, whatever her secrets. He liked Rose and would help her or warn her when he could.

Rose got plenty of leftover food from the kitchen and did not care what the kitchen servants thought. She smiled at them while packing it neatly on a tray, grabbed another bottle of wine under her arm, and was off to her room to see Jessie. When she turned around the corner on her floor from the servants' stairway, she half bumped into Ollie and almost dropped the tray, with them both saving the contents.

"Sir Waters? I thought you said you would be gone for a while?" Feeling flushed and annoyed bumping into him.

"Good evening, Lady Dumont. I believe I did say I might be gone. However, I was just informed that my presence is needed; thus, I will leave early tomorrow morning. Should I assume that your lady friend is still with you?" Looking at her tray and bottle she was carrying.

"Yes, and thank you once again for helping and keeping it a secret." Rose did not want to be caught with all the food after just having a meal and started for her door. For now, Jessie must stay a secret. She stood there like an idiot, not thinking how she would open the door with her hands full. She tried several unsuccessful attempts. She looked at Ollie, who just stood there staring at her and not offering to help and became furious.

Half laughing, he said, "Would you like a hand, Lady Dumont?"

'And why the hell is he being so impish?' Rose was fuming and tried her best to hide her irritation. "Please, sir, and would you hurry in case someone comes!"

Ollie opened the door and stepped inside for Rose to pass. He noticed Jessie sitting on the couch. "Evening Jessie, I hope all is well. Lady Dumont, sorry to leave so soon, but I'm needed downstairs. Evening ladies." Without waiting for any reply, he closed the door and was gone.

"Ah... that darn man can drive me up the wall – he's so irritating!" Rose was trying to balance the bottle and the tray at the table, and Jessie stood up to help.

"What is it with the two of you? Why do you hate the man so?"

"I don't hate him, Jessie. I just can't stand him!" She opened a bottle to pour the wine.

"Why?" Jessie laughed at Rose for being clueless.

Before answering, Rose took a deep breath, "I don't know why, but he reminds me of someone. Being reminded of him is upsetting."

"Oh, your first love that was ended before it could have bloomed."

"No, Jessie – that love would never have bloomed. He would never have done that to his father. It's another story for another day."

Downstairs the king took the opportunity to have a quick word with his son, Philippe. He decided not to prolong the discussion about Rosaline.

Without them noticing, Antoine was listening. Thinking they were private from eavesdropping. Ollie, who sought Philippe out to have a last-minute conversation about his trip at dawn the morrow, also witnessed the whole conversation.

"Son, I must inform you that your betrothal to Lady Rosaline is canceled. You were a second-born child when that was agreed to, except now you will be king. You will have to marry royalty equal to your status."

Philippe looked angry and disappointed. "What will happen to Lady Dumont? Where will she go or stay, and who will she marry?"

"Her father was a good and trusted friend of mine. I will care for her until a proper man offers his hand, or I shall find one myself. Only the best for her, I promise. If it pleases you, you can interrogate him before it's approved."

Philippe said nothing; he looked at his father and nodded, then turned around and walked away. Antoine had to say something and came out of hiding,

"Well, father, I believe you just burst his bubble; he was keen on her." Antoine shared with his father.

"I know, but it had to be said. Now that that's said and done, it's time to find a proper wife for the both of you." His father never bothered to look at him when he spoke. Antoine left without saying a word in return - dreading for that day to come.

Ollie gave Philippe time to breathe and come to terms with what he overheard before approaching him. He didn't take too long; a distraction in the matters of the heart was always a good thing. He should know. '*So, Lady Dumont was open to any marriage - that is good to hear.*' He wondered if Philippe would approve of him to take her hand. What was he thinking? His friend - future king that set his heart on a woman just heard he can't have her, and now he's thinking of taking her for himself! He liked the young lady and found her interesting and very much attractive - but marriage?

"Philippe," he called out.

"Ollie, just the man I was looking for."

Ollie said, "I've come to make sure all is in order for my journey tomorrow and to discuss a few matters before I leave."

"Yes, my friend, just the distraction I need. I will be joining you. Come, let's walk to my study."

While Jessie was eating what Rose brought, she changed into something more comfortable. They both sat in the lounge area with the tray and bottle between them.

"Jessie, you have all my attention. What's this story about 'again'? As far as I know, I was taken once and brought back?"

Jessie thought of how to explain and clarify why her parents kept it from her.

"Well, Rose, you will be shocked to hear this, but please have an open mind. I don't think your parents would approve; however, I think it's time you know what happened to you when you were about three years old."

Rose sat upright with wide eyes waiting patiently.

"You remember the bedtime stories your father told when you were younger and how you lived in them and sometimes corrected him or told a story yourself?"

Rose thought about that. "I remember my father telling me many stories. Please be more specific."

"About the Vikings."

"Yes, but I can't remember correcting him or telling one myself – why? He stopped telling them after a while and refused to say more and spoke about others."

"Well, when you were about three years old, your parents left you with the housekeeper for a few minutes. In those days, when your father went to collect the taxes, your mother used to ride with him. They took this ride together often, but after this incident, she never left your side."

"What happened to me?"

"A group of Vikings raided the town, and you were taken! You were playing outside, waiting for your parents to return home, and the housekeeper was close by when it all happened. The woman said it happened so fast that she freaked out and started shouting, which she regrets because it shocked you into silence. She told me you never uttered a word or sound when they grabbed you.

"The keeper did try to save you, but they hit her unconscious. Your father did everything in his power to follow them. However, he had an unforeseen accident with his horse. Something startled the animal, and your father was thrown off, bumped his head and was knocked out cold. The villagers that decided to help found him an hour later, still dazed. He was severely hurt from the fall.

"By that time, it was too late to find you. Your parents never stopped looking, though. They were in a dreadful state. They rode everywhere looking for you and promising bounty out for your safe return home. You were long gone!"

Rose was pacing now and could not remember any of it.

"But why can't I remember any of this, and why have they not told me? How did I get back if they could not find me?"

"That is a mystery to us all? You were found crying outside by the door. It was still early in the morning; the workers were just waking up. The gardener found you and brought you inside. Your mother decided to color your hair as a minor disguise if they were looking for you and kept you indoors for a long time. She was highly paranoid.

"You kept saying Vikings and pirates that your father decided to tell you stories about them. They believed you were traumatized and tried their best to calm you and make it feel like it was all just a dream. Your father was kind with his words towards them for your sake and hoped nothing bad happened to you. Or something which could cause long-term psychological scars that can affect you one day. You came to believe the stories and said you could live in them the way he told them. You remember that, don't you?"

"Yes, because he was good, not because I remembered something."

"I think you blocked it out. It happens to some when they experience a shock or being badly traumatized."

"I still can't remember! So, my hair was colored because of that event? In case I escaped somehow, and they were looking for me? It all sounds so surreal! If this actually happened, then someone brought me back. There is no way a child of three can leave on her own and return home by herself! How long was I gone for?"

"About two months. They called me the same day to look you over, to see that you were well and not harmed in any way. You seemed fine and still chirpy, content; it's as if you had never left. I told them that you mentally blocked that time out, and it's not a bad thing. You turned out fine. Strangely enough, they retook you. How bizarre does that sound?"

Rose answered, "I still can't get over the fact I was taken at three by Vikings! Have they ever attacked here again after my return home?"

"No, the king put his men all over the land on full security. Your father was head of that security until the war began, and they were all needed to fight somewhere else. They believed they would never return, and they never have – until that day!"

Rose was thinking hard and really wanted to remember that day and what happened to her. Which tribe took her, and who brought her back? She longed for a walk outside to think better. Their wine was finished, and she needed another bottle. The wine was weaker than the Vikings drinks; even so, she felt a little light-headed with the history of her youth. Rose desperately needed another drink, thinking more wine might help to accept what happened and the fact that her parents kept it from her was all too much!

"I'm going to fetch another bottle – you wait here – I'll be back soon."

Rose was ready to leave when Jessie stood up to stop her. "I think it's best if we get some sleep, and tomorrow, we can have another walk and talk some more. Don't make me sorry for telling you this." Jessie could see Rose was slightly tipsy and upset.

"No, I'm grateful you told me – I just need to get out for a while. I promise I'll be back soon." She left before Jessie could protest.

In the kitchen, Rose was staring around, not remembering why she came down. She decided to go outside and stood there for a while, enjoying the fresh air. She heard someone approach and turned.

"You again! Are you following me? Never mind... I'm really not in the mood for your teasing or flirting, whatever you are trying to accomplish with me." Rose turned back to her thoughts.

Ollie could see something was bothering her and she looked stressed out.

"Is there something I can help you with, Lady Dumont?"

"No - no one can help me!" Rose felt lost and confused. When will she ever feel whole again?

Ollie asked again, "I can try if you'll let me?"

Rose was about to spill it all by saying, '*Can you give my memories back or my parents or a life I so want, but am not allowed to have.*' However, being tipsy, when she turned, ready to attack him with all her frustration, she turned too fast and lost her balance.

He caught her in his arms. Ollie held on to her and smelled the wine on her breath. Still holding her, he said, "Should I accompany you back to your room or call your friend to help?"

Rose pulled away from him, "No, you imbecile - I'm not drunk!" Then realized she was a little woozy - it must have been the fresh air that hit her. Ollie was still holding her by the arm in case she fell, "Unhand me this instant!" She pushed herself out of his arms just to feel dizzy again, and him saving her from slipping once again.

Rose looked forlorn and guilty. She looked up at him and apologized, "I'm so sorry, Sir Waters, my actions are not my own, and I'm never this rude to anyone. I just don't understand my life – do you understand?"

Ollie was still holding on to her and was fascinated with this beauty in front of him. Her gorgeous eyes were huge, and she looked troubled. He thought about her question and answered, "I guess or should say I believe everyone goes through that at some point in their lives where life makes no sense and wonder why they even exist."

"Yes, exactly! That's where I am – lost! Belong nowhere or to no one."

Ollie did not want to take advantage of a drunk woman; however, he could not stop himself. He was bold with his move and slowly leaned down and kissed her. To his surprise, she kissed him back. Before the kiss could intensify, he stopped and was expecting a slap, which never came. At the very least, he considered that she might never speak to him again, yet it was done on an impulse he could not resist.

Rose, for her part, was speechless; her head was still spinning; she was shocked by her reaction to the kiss – she actually enjoyed it!

Ollie was waiting for any ill words for his brave move from her, which never came, so he spoke up, "I think I should return you to your room, milady." He politely offered his arm so she could be steady, and she accepted. At her bedroom door, all Rose said was thank you, then went straight inside. She was not sure what she was feeling at that moment. She could not think what to say to him and was thankful that he wasn't his talkative self. When she entered her room, Jessie was beside herself and noticed Rose was flushed.

"Are you alright, Rose? You had me worried – I almost came looking for you!"

"I'm fine; I think you were right about sleeping." Rose walked without stopping to her bed and fell onto it. Jessie climbed in next to her. There was always a candle burning through the night for some light.

"Jessie?"

"Yes, Rose?"

Half whispering and half asleep, Rose asked, "Are there any other bits of news that you know of that was not told, or they forgot to tell me or refused to tell me? Any more shocking news I should be aware of before I pass out?"

There was one more, but she was not sure if she should tell her. Jessie was a firm believer in telling the truth, and Rose should know what awaits or what's expected of her. Jessie could never understand why her parents could not tell her. By not telling her, it made Rose look weak, and she was not. She decided to spill so Rose can sort them out as she pleases.

"Yes, there is, just one. You have been betrothed to Philippe for a long time." Jessie waited for a response.

"Oh, is that all?" Rose said and was fast asleep.

Jessie was sure that that one did not sink in, and she'd have an earful in the morning when it did, then she would have to explain once again.

Jessie was an early riser and started to clean the leftover food and empty bottles from the living area. She stacked them neatly on a tray for the servant to take away. While Jessie was tidying up the room, Clara walked in and was surprised to find Jessie there. The stranger did not look like any of the castle servants, not to mention that she has never seen her around the castle before. Clara was upset and started throwing questions at her.

"Who are you? Has the lady got a new handmaiden? Lady Rosaline has not called me for almost two days now. Are you new here? I have never seen you before."

Jessie was hesitant to answer, so she politely explained that she was hired two days ago to be a personal helper. For more information, she must speak to the lady herself. Jessie asked her to bring a pot of tea for Lady Dumont for when she awakes. She wanted to ask her to bring breakfast as well, yet would not dare.

Clara had nothing more to say and took the tray and left. Jessie went to the bedroom area to hide behind the curtains and stayed there in case any more unwelcome company entered. The curtains closed up most of the bedroom area where Rose could dress in private as well. There was much hidden from the prying eyes of visitors. The room was divided in two from the bedroom and lounge area. There was a single couch nearby the bed where Jessie was sitting, watching Rose sleep. Even though she would be queen one day, she was still so innocent, Jessie worried for her.

Clara came and left again, so Jessie went through to pour herself a cup of tea. This hiding act was becoming tedious and too much for her. Being stuck here inside the room was not healthy at all. She missed her small cottage; even though she asked a local kid to keep an eye on her animals, she hoped they were still well. She promised to pay and gave him a little something up-front, yet she would reward him handsomely when she returned.

Her steed was well cared for by a stableman, something she did not have to worry about. She had to pay upfront for this service due to distrust; at least he could be trusted with animals. Jessie knew she had to leave soon but was worried about how Rose would react to the news. She decided to stay for one more day and then be on her way; she would inform Rose when the time was right.

Jessie was lost in thought while standing at the balcony entrance – not wanting to go too far out to be noticed. She did not hear the door open and close or hear someone enter the room. When he spoke, she spilled her tea with fright.

Antoine said, "Sorry, I never meant to startle you. Where is Lady Rosaline?" Not coming straight out and asking who she was.

"Good day, milord. Lady Dumont is still asleep - should I wake her?"

"No, it's fine. Do I know you? You look awfully familiar?"

"No, milord, we have never met before."

"Well, you look like someone I've met before or seen recently."

Just then, Rose opened the curtains and yawned. The voices woke her up and was surprised to find Antoine in her room.

"Good day, Antoine. To what do I owe the pleasure of such an early visit?"

Jessie went over to pour Rose a cup of tea and handed it to her, upon which Rose asked politely, "Would you like a cup of tea, Antoine?"

"No, thank you, Rose. I thought I'd invite you for a walk or a picnic later if you are interested in going out. That's if you have no other engagements?"

Rose's facial expression changed immediately, remembering the last words Jessie spoke before she passed out. *'Engagements!'* She stared at Jessie, and Jessie realized that the information had sunk in. Rose shot up to face Jessie. Rose could not help herself and blurted it out, "I'm betrothed to Philippe - since when?"

Jessie and Antoine stared at each other and then at Rose. Antoine sat down and said nothing, so Jessie went on to explain, "For a long time, and before you go asking more

71

questions, your parents were too scared to tell you. It was about two full moons before you became ill and were taken, there was a ball at the castle, and you were going to be formally introduced to your future husband as well. However, as you know, on the day when you were all leaving, I heard the measles were spreading and stopped you beforehand, then everything changed."

"Oh, just like that! No notice or anything! Not that I don't like Philippe, but a warning would have sufficed."

Rose remembered that day well, indeed the day when her whole life began to change. However, she could not understand why her parents were scared to tell her. She couldn't even think how her life would have been now if the measles had not killed everyone she loved. She would have been engaged by now or even married – a princess, and to top it all, she would have never met Popi and the Viking clan she came to love dearly. She couldn't even compare the two lives she would have had. Rose thought about the other people she would never have known if nothing changed. But there was one crucial thing, more than anything; she wished that her parents were still alive!

"Oh, Rose, your parents were just looking out for you. I don't think it would have happened straight away, with your father gone all the time. They would have asked Philippe to call and court you before any real arrangements were made. They wanted you to be happy."

Rose sat down again. "I know Jessie, coming back and hearing all this is too much. I'm not angry, just confused. I still love and miss my parents so much!" Rose looked at Antoine, and he looked pale.

"Oh lord, what are you hiding from me too? Please tell me, so I don't make a fool of myself, or I will never leave this room again!"

Antoine spoke up, "Your betrothal is canceled. He was not next in line to be king then, and now that he is, things have changed. My father explained this to Philippe for the first time last night. He too believed it was still on and was distraught with the news." Antoine felt sorry for Rose.

"Oh. Well, that settles it then." Everyone was quiet for a while before Rose answered, "A walk and picnic sounds inviting; thank you for thinking of me. Would you mind if my friend can accompany us?" She did not want to think further on the matter and sought to forget it all.

Antoine and Jessie were relieved not to discuss the matter further. They both let it rest with Jessie being the first to speak up, "No, Rose, that's fine. I'll wait until you get back."

Looking at them, Antoine could not help but wonder what the association was. The woman called Rose by name, not by a formal title like 'Lady' or 'Miss' Rosaline.

"It's no problem; you are welcome to join. It will just be the three of us, but first, tell me who you are because this feeling that you seem familiar is eating at me and that I know you from somewhere!"

Rose trusted Antoine and knew that he could keep a secret, except Jessie's one was hers to be told by Jessie alone. Rose would never betray her friend's trust or put her in any unnecessary harm.

She looked at Jessie, then at Antoine, and explained, "This is Jessie from Chinon, where I lived. She was our healer in town and a very close member of our family, the only one I have left, and the only link I have to special memories of my parents. We want to keep her visit a secret, so if you can, please don't tell anyone!" Rose begged.

"That I can do." He didn't understand why it should be a secret —nonetheless— "Any friend of yours is a friend of mine. I don't understand why, though? A healer would be welcomed in the castle; still, I swear I've seen you before?"

"For now, that is what we want, and no, she has never been to the castle before. Perhaps on your travels, you passed her by, which is triggering a memory?"

"You may be right; it could be that. Fine then – I'll see you both out front in an hour if that is enough time for you to get ready?"

"Plenty, thank you, Antoine."

Before he saw himself out, he turned to Jessie and said, "And Jessie, if we are all going to be friends on a first-name basis, please call me Antoine."

Jessie smiled at him, and when he was gone, the two women just stared at each other.

Rose met Antoine in front while Jessie went ahead towards the kitchen exit, saying she would meet them there. Antoine found this secrecy and sneaking very entertaining. Today Rose had no choice but to dress formally in proper attire, seeing that everyone noticed she was accompanying Prince Antoine for a picnic. Rose showed him where she and Jessie usually sit; it was a perfect spot for a picnic, especially away from prying eyes.

When they arrived, Jessie was already there. Antoine laid out the blanket and unpacked the basket, he had enough food and wine packed for four people, and they enjoyed the meal while having a relaxed conversation.

Rose and Jessie were having flashbacks of her parents and how disobedient she was at times. They were all laughing and enjoying the day. It was still bugging Antoine that he somehow knew her. Jessie's face was familiar – it was haunting.

Jessie felt relaxed with Antoine; she thought he was a decent man and found him very easy to talk to. She could see Rose liked and trusted him because she spoke openly about her Viking days on the island, and Antoine was listening with enthusiasm. Rose started by saying how Antoine reminded her of Cnut. They weren't the same person, yet their qualities were close. Antoine was intrigued by her stories and asked many questions on the matter. He was surprised by how civil they were. Rose informed them that not all tribes like change and that some still clung to their old ways.

Rose felt relaxed and was enjoying the company; she even made plans to go for a long ride the next day and have a picnic at a different location. She was excited about the thought. Antoine agreed and asked if he could bring a friend and said that he could be trusted. He swore his life on it. Rose approved; she knew him as well, as his assistant, Léo, who helped her with the water-well. Jessie thought to tell Rose now rather than later that she will be leaving early tomorrow morning.

"No, Jessie, you can't leave so soon? We still have so much catching up to do!"

"My sweet Rose, I have duties that are waiting for me, and I can't neglect my animals again. The last time I left without thought, some of my animals ran off, and several died. It was sad at the time. Now that I know you are safe and healthy, I can breathe again. Perhaps Antoine can bring you to visit for a few days, and we can go visit your parent's graves together?" Jessie looked at Antoine for verification.

"I would love a long trip once more, and we can make it a joy ride. How many rooms do you have?" Honestly not thinking about what he said.

Jessie just stared at him and laughed, "Only one!" She felt the need to be more specific about her living. "It's a cottage out in the fields in the middle of nowhere!"

Antoine never blinked an eye – it did not bother him. "That's fine; I shall bring a tent to sleep in. I can't wait to go." He seemed excited and did not care about her status at all. He accepted Jessie as she was.

Jessie felt that this man was her half-brother, and if they had grown up together, they would have been very close.

"OK, you guys..." Rose laughed at Antoine. "We can plan that, and yes, I would love to visit my birth home and my parent's graves. But please, Jessie, bless me with one more day in your presence, and I'll see you off myself. We will ride with you for a while to send you on your journey – please!" Rose begged and pulled a sad face that made Jessie laugh.

"OK, one more day! You are impossible, my dove." They all laughed. Antoine could see the closeness and love that was shared between them and envied their friendship. He wished he had something as dear as theirs; other than Léo, he had his brother as well, but it still wasn't the same closeness.

They packed up and started walking back. This time they all walked to the back entrance with Jessie, where Antoine dropped the empty picnic basket in the kitchen and escorted them through the servant's stairwell to Rose's room. Inside they made plans for the next day and what should be in the picnic basket. Antoine said he would handle the basket and the horses; all they had to do was be at the stables on time. He saw himself out. The two women went to lie down to catch a quick nap before lunch.

When they woke up, Clara was in the room. Rose walked through to ask her to bring food for two and a pot of tea for lunch, and when it was time, to bring the supper up with two bottles of wine. Rose noticed that Clara looked irritated, but could not be bothered by how the helper felt right now or wonder why. She decided to stay in and talk to Jessie. There was still much to tell her, and talking about her adopted family on the island actually helped Rose cope with her loss. She still

77

missed them so much and knew she was missed too. Rose wished them all well.

By the time they finished their supper, Rose had finished with her story. She wasn't sure if she should tell Jessie about her attacker and that she killed him – not on purpose; it was a reaction – she decided not to. Jessie did not have to know that part. Both felt content, relaxed with their own thoughts with a cup of tea.

Later, when they were resting in bed, Jessie eventually explained her journey to find her and how she had spoken to Philippe when he came to the inn looking for recruits. She told Rose that he was worried and had done all he could and sent word out for any information about her disappearance.

Rose was listening with one eye open, and after Jessie finished explaining, Rose was fast asleep.

Jessie was staring at the ceiling; her mind was full of thoughts that she could not sleep. Now that the marriage was canceled, Rose had to decide what she wanted to do with her life or perhaps choose whom to marry. She had so much going for her, and she could do anything her heart desired.

Rose needed a man who could support her and would definitely understand her, and most importantly, love her unconditionally. Jessie made a promise to her father and failed. This time around, she would do everything in her power to see that Rose gets everything she deserves for her future happiness. She would have been queen one day – now her future was uncertain.

4

*A*ntoine woke with a fright; he realized who Jessie reminded him of – his deceased brother Louis the Second – but how could that be? How could she resemble his blood – unless...?

He heard a little about his father's active, youthful days. His father must have had an affair with her mother some years ago. She is much older than his brother Louis would have been, so it was before his parents met or married. He guessed her age and did the math. To be sure, he would have to ask her age without sounding suspicious. He will not share this with his lover Léo until he was sure. Maybe that's why Jessie did not want to be seen or noticed in the castle – in case his father noticed her as well. Antoine wondered what he'd do about that if he did?

Antoine met the two women in the stables as planned. Their horses were saddled and ready – Antoine packed the picnic basket on Léo's horse. He could not help but steal a glimpse now and then after the realization of his new finding. Knowing what he comprehended, he looked at her with fresh eyes; the resemblance between the two was uncanny. He decided to ignore it for now and enjoy their ride. He introduced Léo to Jessie, and they were off. They left the castle grounds and rode down to a river not far off to have their picnic. The day went exceptionally well, and they were all having fun.

Rose felt free again and took the opportunity to swim; everyone started laughing and saying she was mad. Not long, the two men dared each other to join her - and so they did! There was much laughter and shouting. Their picnic was almost at an end; they were all relaxing under the shade after their activities. Rose and Léo passed out, which left Antoine and Jessie to themselves. It was peaceful and quiet while Antoine was thinking of a way to talk to her that didn't sound like he was snooping for answers.

"Today was entertaining and fun. Trust these two to pass out on us!" he laughed.

"It truly was, thank you!"

"It's a pleasure." It was the perfect time to query her on her life and asked, "May I ask you a few personal questions about your nationality? I'm just curious, but if you do mind, then that's OK. I won't feel offended. Not many people like to talk about their lives or the past."

Jessie thought about it and thought it was harmless enough. If it got too personal, she would tell him and gave an approving nod in answer.

"Good, where do you come from, and who taught you to be a healer?"

Innocent enough, she explained her tribe and about her mother, that she was a healer and passed it on to her at a certain age. Jessie went on to explain that she had been married, and with her husband's passing, she decided to explore life over here, teaching and helping others with the healing powers as her mother did. Antoine was listening intently. He asked where her mother was now and if she was still alive – her answer was yes. Her mother was unhappy when she left their tribe, but she hopes to see her people soon in the future.

"How old are you?" he asked bluntly.

Jessie stared at him, and he laughed, "I'm sorry, it just popped out! I know you should never ask one's age, although I am curious."

She felt uneasy and gave him an answer, "I'm thirty-five!"

So, it was a few years before his father married, and it took his mother almost a year to conceive their first child. Is it possible that Jessie could be his half-sister? He must find out the truth and would love to get to know her better. Did she know? If he asked her outright, would she be shocked? So many questions were flooding his mind. He decided to leave it for now as there would be many more opportunities to ask when they spent more time together.

"Are you still leaving tomorrow? About what time, so we can meet and ride out with you as planned?"

The other two woke up, stretching and yawning. "Welcome back, sleepy heads," Antoine said to them.

Jessie answered, "Very early. I don't want to take too long to get back home. There is much to do when I return."

They agreed to meet at a specific time in the morning. They packed up and returned to the castle.

Their last night together was tranquil. Now that Jessie was leaving, and Rose promised to see her soon, there was not much to say. They spoke of the old days and about her parents and were early in bed for Jessie's sake.

The following day, Jessie went to fetch her horse where she left him when first arriving and paid the keeper what she still owed, then returned to the stables where the rest were waiting. Léo was not joining but came down to say his goodbyes to Jessie and wished her a safe trip home. When they left, it was just starting to get light and a perfect day for traveling. There was a cool, calm wind in the air and a promise of rain perhaps later that evening. Hopefully, by that time, Jessie would reach an inn to settle before the rain started.

They trotted with Jessie for almost an hour before they said their final goodbyes with Rose in tears. Jessie felt sad too but fought them back. However, when she was alone on the road, she allowed them to fall.

Antoine noticed that they were being followed but said nothing to the women. He could see they were guards from the castle and thought they were there to see to their safety for being so far off the castle grounds. They were not on the road, but further up riding between the trees, hoping not to be noticed. What was confusing was when they returned home, they were nowhere to be seen; he thought nothing further of it and escorted Rose for breakfast when they entered the castle. Rose felt lonely once again; however, she was grateful for Antoine's friendship this time around.

Philippe and Ollie were on their way home with their escorts. They finished their business early and were satisfied with their assignment. It was a day after Jessie left the castle. She was not pushing her horse too much because he was old. Jessie came to an inn that night and settled down just when the rain started pouring down. She felt that something was amiss or forgot to say something to Rose or left something behind; the feeling was unsettling. She tried to put that aside and slept soundly that night.

She had breakfast and was off at first light. She was sure she was being followed, but who and why would someone follow her? Jessie thought she was being paranoid and tried to push it out of her mind.

In the late afternoon, Jessie decided she might just as well camp outside if the weather persisted. So far, it was a beautiful evening. She could hear running water and looked for a perfect spot to settle down and made a small fire. Jessie left her steed freely to eat the overgrown grass and quench his thirst with the fresh stream water. After she ate something small and feeling content, she laid down and closed her eyes. Not long, she heard footsteps close by, and when she opened her eyes, she found two men standing over her.

On the course towards home after collecting the taxes, Ollie noticed a horse crossing their path and wondered where the owner was; it looked old and tired. Philippe also wondered and thought it was an ambush. He warned his troops, and with wary eyes, they moved closer. Philippe and Ollie dismounted and walked towards the horse with their swords drawn, expecting the worst. Philippe motioned everyone to stop and keep quiet so they could hear any sounds of oncoming horses or footsteps – there were none. Ollie was sure he heard something further in, sounded like a moan or cry. He heard running water and went further in with his sword, prepared for a fight. Close to the water, he saw a woman lying on the ground and went closer.

"Ma'am, are you OK?" Ollie called out. "Are you in trouble?"

She said nothing, and the moans became louder. When Ollie got closer, he noticed who it was and ran to her side. "Good heavens, Jessie! Who did this to you?" Jessie had been stabbed numerous times and left for dead. She had lost a lot of blood; it was a miracle that she was still alive. Her words were mumbled. Ollie said, "I can't understand you - try to talk slower." All he could make out was 'castle,' which made no sense to him.

Philippe came closer to see who it was. "I know her! She approached me once at an inn to discuss Rosaline's disappearance. She was their healer. Why would anyone kill her?"

Ollie looked around. "Well, milord, what I can see, it was not a robbery - all her belongings are still here. It was done deliberately. Someone was out to get her!"

"Do you think she can be saved?" Philippe asked. "I think there might be someone that could perhaps help her, but he's close to the next inn."

"No, she will never make the trip." Ollie felt sorry for Jessie, and Rosaline was going to be devastated when she hears this.

Jessie was trying to say something else; he put his ear closer to her lips. She spoke slowly and forced the words out for him to understand. "Please protect our Rose." Those were her last words with her last breath; she was limp in his arms.

Ollie made that promise to her and whispered, "I promise I shall, and I will avenge your death too." He was infuriated. He stood up, took her blanket, and covered her with it. He fetched her horse and laid her across to take her to Rosaline for a proper burial.

"We are taking her with?" Philippe asked, "We can just as well bury her here."

Ollie was hesitant to tell him but decided Philippe should understand what she meant to Rosaline and why she would want Jessie to be buried properly.

"Prince Philippe, she came from the castle. I believe she was on her way home." Philippe was about to ask a question when Ollie lifted his hands to say he was not finished and that he was going to explain. "She went to see Lady Dumont and was visiting there in secret this whole time. They asked me to keep it a secret and seeing how they were together and how happy they were, I decided to let them be. Who was I to interfere? They were close at some point, and with my brief encounter of their reunion, I believe Lady Dumont would want her there, not buried in a field somewhere where she was murdered." Ollie expected Philippe to be a little angry at this news and surprised him by saying nothing.

Philippe ordered his troops to pack up her belonging and put it on the horse with the deceased woman. They were silent for a while when they returned to the road.

"When did she arrive at the castle?" Philippe was curious to know why he was not entrusted with her secret. He would have kept it for as long as Rosaline desired to keep her there.

"She arrived at the time of the ball," Ollie answered and explained further how he found her hiding in the bushes and what he did to help.

Their ride back was in haste this time. They wanted the body to be attended to before it started to stink. Both men were dreading facing Rose with this horrible incident. It was not going to be easy seeing her break down. Philippe wondered how much more must the poor girl endure...

They arrived around supper time the next day. Everyone was in the main hall, waiting to be called in to eat. Ollie and Philippe looked glum at their entrance. The king saw their mood, walked over and asked how the meeting went; Philippe said fine.

The king asked, "You had me worried! Then why do you look like your best horse died?"

Philippe looked at his father and thought not to tell him until he tells Rosaline first. His words would not be so kind to the death of a peasant or understand their relationship or what Rosaline might be feeling. He noticed that his brother Antoine and Rosaline grew close on his departure. He was happy about that. They had not noticed them enter yet.

When Rose turned and saw Ollie, she thought of their kiss and smiled, but when she saw the look he gave her, she went ice-cold and wondered what came over him. Philippe came closer to greet them and asked if he could have a word with her. They all stood in the corridor just outside the door. Ollie was standing on one side while Philippe started explaining what happened.

"I'm so sorry, Rosaline!"

"What? No... No! That can't be true – no, it's not true – no, I just saw her, why would she be dead?" Rose was trying to understand this tragedy. She looked at Ollie; maybe he can enlighten her and say it's not true. He looked at her and nodded. The look of sorrow in his eyes said it all. She screamed and fell to her knees, "No...! Why...? How did this happen?" Crying and trying to understand why she had to lose the one person she had left who was connected to her parents. The only lifeline of a family she had left on this land. Now she, too, was gone! "Where is she?"

"Still in the stables, we sent for the priest, and then she'll be carried off to the church as soon as possible."

Rose was up and ran out the door to where they were keeping Jessie's body - Antoine came out worried after someone said they heard a scream. "What's going on here?"

"Come walk with us brother, I will explain on the way, and I have a few questions for you too?" Philippe answered.

"What - Jessie's dead, but how? Was she robbed?"

"No, all her belongings were still with her," answered Ollie. He wished he knew what happened here when they left. Why did Jessie want to hide and not be seen, and whatever the reason was, she was found out by this person and killed for it? Ollie had to find a way to speak to Rosaline in private. She must have all the answers, knowing why Jessie was hiding. Whatever the reason, it got her killed, and he wanted to know why.

Antoine pulled Philippe to one side and said, "I need to talk to you in private. Please come to my chambers after supper or when all this is sorted out."

"What's this about?"

"All this! I might have an idea who was involved, and you are not going to like what I have to say."

"Fine, I'll be there as soon as I can."

The priest came; Philippe spoke to him and gave him a pouch of coins. The priest blessed the body where Rose was sitting and crying, holding her dear friend. She saw the disgust in the priest's eyes and that he was not happy blessing an Indian woman that was not Catholic. Rose decided to find out how to do it on her own so that it pleased her friend in her afterlife, or whatever Jessie believed in. Rose would not have the priest's false prayers fall on her friend. Before they removed Jessie's body, she needed to talk to someone. Antoine and Philippe were busy, so she went over to Ollie.

"Ollie, can you please help me with something?"

"Yes, of course, milady, whatever you ask!"

"Please tell me you know something about how an Indian would go about to bury a loved one?" Hoping he knew.

"There are many ways; different tribes have different beliefs – they all vary. Which tribe did Jessie belong to?"

"I believe she belonged to the Sioux tribe."

"They all believe in burying their deceased out in the open. Many believe in placing food and objects close to the body for their afterlife. Most importantly, you will have to place an eagle feather on the body; they believe that the eagle is a sacred bird. Most tribes believe that after death begins a new life – reborn into which way you lived. It can be an insect, animal or water creature, or even a plant or tree. Because she was murdered and not of natural causes, you need to find peace for her soul before sending her off. It will take at least four days of doing this."

"How do I do this?" By this time, the two brothers were listening as well.

"Well, first, you will have to wash her body and wrap her tightly in robes or a new blanket and place her in an open casket. You will have to start a fire close to the coffin and stay with her for at least four days while people come to pay their respects and place gifts and food for her journey. It should be a peaceful area. You can burn her next, or you may bury her with the closed casket.

"Most don't bury the dead underground because wild animals will smell their flesh, dig it up and devour it. Thus, they are burnt rather. You have a casket, and we have people who can dig deep, so it's fine. They also believed that when you place a deceased on a horse to carry them to the desired area, you should kill the horse and bury it with the deceased to carry them further in the afterlife."

"I am not killing a horse! We can use a carriage to carry her and her casket, and we shall lead the horse." Rose said firmly. "No more unnecessary deaths." It was weird to listen to him explain Jessie's beliefs; they were almost the same as the Vikings. Rose wondered what gods she believed in and wondered why she had never asked her? There were many questions Rose wished she had asked Jessie. She never thought that their time together would end so abruptly.

Antoine said, "We can help with whatever you want or need to do this properly for your friend." He looked sad. He wanted to say *whatever for my sister* but could not. It was still just a hunch he had, yet he was sure of it. She must have told Rose; he will ask her later at an appropriate time.

Philippe thanked the priest and sent him off; he said they would see to her themselves. He did not argue the fact and was happy to leave. Philippe wondered, "How do you know so much about the Indians?"

"I had a friend that was one, and I lived with them for a few weeks. It felt like home!" No one understood what he meant by that, and he did not elaborate further on the subject.

Rose said, "Tell me, will it matter if an outsider does this ritual? What happens if it goes wrong, and she wanders in the afterlife or something else that is bad?" Remembering that she could never participate in the Viking burial rituals because of their superstitions.

"I believe you will do it right for your friend; she was family of yours, and that counts. Your heart is in the right place, no matter the outcome." Ollie was sincere.

All she wanted to do was embrace him and thank him for those kind words. Not just him, but Philippe and Antoine, too, for understanding and wanting to help.

Rose wanted to know more about what happened to Jessie; she still had many questions. She was still standing close to Ollie and moved closer and half-whispered, "Ollie, do you think she suffered? Was she in much pain?"

Ollie was not sure he should share this information. It will break her more. "I think it's best not to tell you, milady. For your own sake, it's best not to know."

"Was she still alive when you found her?"

Ollie thought for a while before answering, "Yes."

Tears started swimming in her eyes, "What did she say to you?"

"Milady..." he didn't want to hurt her further and wished she would stop asking him these questions.

But before he could protest, she chipped in, "Please, Ollie! I need to know!"

He also, for some reason, whispered and said, "Her last words to me were... *Please protect our Rose.*"

The tears started running down her cheeks, the pain of her friend suffering and her name being mentioned with her last breath, still trying to protect her.

Rose, arms crossed over her chest, leaned her forehead on Ollie's chest and cried. He felt uncomfortable and looked at Antoine and Philippe, who was listening and watching the whole scene. He lifted one arm and pulled her closer to console her.

After securing the body, Rose was escorted to her room, where she cried herself to sleep. Jessie was all Rose had left as a family. Now she too had passed.

Philippe made a turn to his brothers' room to hear what he had to say about Jessie's death. Antoine told him about the two men that followed them at her departure and weren't seen again when they turned back to the castle. He said he thought nothing of it at the time, and the men belonged to their father. He informed Philippe who he thought Jessie was and the affair their father might have had with her mother long before he married their mother. He said that Jessie resembled Louis, their deceased brother, in many ways.

Thinking about it now, Philippe agreed, yet they would have to make sure of it somehow. Perhaps even ask Rose if it was true. If it were, why would their father have her murdered? What was so wrong to have a child with another woman? Was it because she was half Indian and he was embarrassed or was he just plain evil?

When Philippe left with all this information, he was not sure what to do about it. What could he do anyway? It was his father, the king, who arranged for an innocent woman, perhaps his own daughter – to be condemned to death.

His father was seeking them out to ask what all this mayhem was about in his castle, and Philippe told him, "Rose's close friend was murdered on the way to her home. She is in a state, and we are helping her to send her off."

"What do you mean to send her off? Can't the priest just bury her and get it over with?" King Louis was irritated with the fuss over this peasant woman.

"Are you not going to ask who this friend was, father? No, it means a lot to Rosaline to do it right! They were very close, so I hear." He looked at his father in a different light.

"I was getting there, was just wondering why not do it as we always do through the church. If Lady Dumont insists on doing it differently, I will show my respect as king and show face for Rosaline's sake. Who was she?"

"She was their healer when her parents were alive. I hear she was part of the family. There's no need to show your face, father. It's not close by, and it's a ritual that must be done properly. I will tell her you to send your regards." Philippe turned and walked away.

*R*ose was alone during the bathing stage of her friend. There was no one else that would help or that she would allow to help. She first washed the body and cried at all the stabbed marks she saw. With loving touches, she rubbed scented oils before covering Jessie with a blanket she received from Antoine. When Rose was done and ready to let go after breaking down many times, a man came to carry the body and placed Jessie in her casket, made in rapid time. Rose led the horse to 'their' spot right under the huge tree, where they went twice for a picnic. It was a peaceful and beautiful area.

They took the casket off the carriage and placed it gently under the tree with Jessie inside. Rose made a fire with additional logs to last for four days. Ollie was there helping with the instructions. The night when Rose was taken to her room after securing the body in a safe place, Ollie went in search of an eagle's feather. He was lucky to find one who kept an eagle as a pet. It was a beautiful feather, and he placed it on Jessie's chest before adding a loaf of bread, cheese, and a bottle of wine to the casket. With it, a small knife he took from the kitchen.

Rose placed all Jessie's belongings she had on her at the time. It's said it was a good thing; the belongings she would need are the things she needed on her travels when she was alive. Rose sat down and waited; there was nothing else to do. There was no one else coming to pay their respects. Ollie will stay with her and protect Rose while she was out in the open – Philippe asked it. However, he would have done it without anyone's request.

Much later, Antoine and Léo came over with more food and placed it in the casket too. With them, they brought a picnic basket to feed them all and two tents, one for Rose and the other for the men to sleep in. Ollie said he had a bedroll and was happy to sleep close to the fire.

During this ritual, Antoine decided it was the least he could do for his sister to show his respect and help ease her spirit to pass on. He did not really understand this method, yet he would comply – for Rose's sake and for Jessie to find peace. The people that were here loved Jessie as long as they knew her and their thoughts were kind. That is all Rose could ask for and appreciated them for their consideration.

95

The next morning, Philippe brought fresh food for them. Rose set fresh flowers with Jessie each day so she would know they were from her. She could think of nothing else to give her but love, and how do you send that?

Antoine walked with Philippe to fetch more wine and food for later. Philippe explained the talk he had with their father and told him not to come for the ritual because it had to be done right. It would be wrong for a man who ordered someone's death to attend the funeral. If this were for Jessie's spirit to pass in peace, his presence would have most probably turned her soul into a wandering ghost! They laughed at the thought, not disrespecting the dead, but it was likely.

On the third day, two men were ordered to dig a deep hole. It took them most of the afternoon to finish. On the fourth, she was placed in the hole with a loose lid on top; Ollie said it was customary for the soul to travel and not be trapped. Rose said her goodbyes and said how much she would be missed and cried again as she had done for the past three nights. She had not cried in front of them again since hearing the news, leaving the tears for her tent when she retired.

Everyone said something before the same two men who had carried Jessie and dug the grave, started filling the hole again. Rose hugged them all for being there for her and Jessie and said she hoped it worked. They packed up all their belongings, packed them on the same carriage Jessie was on and returned to the castle. When Rose got in, she ordered a bath and thought about what her next move would be.

She knew the castle life was not for her anymore, and after losing Jessie, she felt more lost than ever before. Rose knew that they would always care for her at the castle, but she felt trapped – blessed to have caring friends but still trapped in a life she did not want to be in.

5

Rose went about her days in a trance. Once a week, she would walk and place flowers under the tree where Jessie was buried. She went down to eat her meals, smiled at everyone, and spoke to whoever wanted to talk to her. She went out with people on their group picnics and sat there politely, not joining in the games they had planned for the day. Antoine tried his best to help her out of her depression, to be herself again – nothing worked. Rose was acting like a proper lady and kept to herself most days.

A month went by, and Antoine was frustrated with this new woman. He tried everything to change her mood, and still, nothing worked - she was despondent all the time. He needed to help her somehow. Thus, he planned an outing, which might help Rose face her pain and accept her destiny whatever path she takes.

Antoine went to her room after he had a meeting with his father and brother. It was a shocker what his father suggested! They argued before he stormed out. Antoine's plans would not only help Rose but help him, too, to escape from all the drama at the castle. He hoped Rose was up for an adventure.

"Son, I have come to the conclusion that I think will help all involved," King Louis spoke to his sons, "I am still looking for a wife for you, Philippe; there are many proposals. I haven't decided on one yet. We can discuss that some other time. Antoine, I see you and Rosaline are fond of each other. We can still keep her here as planned and marry one of my sons, which will be you." He thought his son would be happy with the idea of marrying Rosaline.

"What? No! You can't decide that for us! I refuse to marry her; she will find a proper suitor on her own time." Antoine would never do that to her. Rose needed someone who could love her and give her things that he knew he could never give her.

"What do you mean you refuse? How can you refuse me?" The king was angry with Antoine's outburst.

"Rosaline needs someone who can make her happy, and I know I can never do that!"

Philippe wasn't sure if Antoine would announce his attraction to the same sex; he spoke up, "He's right, father, they are only friends, and she needs their friendship to be just that. With everything she has gone through, the matters of the heart are another thing. You can't force them to marry and perhaps be happy with the outcome. She needs a different kind of man, not that Antoine is the wrong man, but her views on love are different. We say this not out of disrespect to you, father, but we know her better than you do, and we all want her to be happy one day, especially after all she's been through."

Antoine was thankful for his brothers' speech. His father listened and agreed with him, then without another word, Antoine stormed out.

He took a breather before knocking on Rose's door. She was having tea on her balcony and called out for whoever was knocking to enter.

"Good day, Rose. I have great news, maybe even fantastic news if you hear what I've got to say."

Rose could see something was bothering him. "Is everything alright, Antoine?"

"Yes, I'm fine; don't you want to know what the news is?"

She gave a light laugh, "Yes, of course, please do share!" She invited him to sit.

"Well, we made plans to go to your birth home once and visit... um... you know, and I thought perhaps we can still do it – what do you say? The trip will be fun, and I believe that we can both use the time away from this place."

Rose's heart was aching. Their planned trip was to visit Jessie at her place, and that made her sad. On the other hand, she thought it was an excellent idea.

"When will this happen?" She smiled and agreed to the trip.

"As soon as possible." Not wanting to waste time, he went further to say, "How about early tomorrow morning? Can you pack and be ready so soon? I can handle all the other necessary traveling arrangements."

"I will be ready and can't wait." After losing her dear friend, Rose felt a spark of life returning to her for the first time.

After bidding Rose a good day, Antoine, with a skip in his step, went down to the kitchen, gave orders regarding their food parcels and many bottles of wine. He then went to the stables to give instructions that he wanted two horses ready and attached to a carriage before dawn the next day. Antoine then went to his room to pack what he needed for the trip and made a mental note of what they might still need for outdoor camping – blankets and tents included. There was much to be done! He was feeling the excitement for the trip and could not wait to leave. While he was packing, Philippe came to see him.

"Were you going to tell father about your sex life?" Philippe was worried about how close he came to announce it.

"No, he just took me by surprise and made me angry with that statement. You know I want Rose happy, and I'm certainly not the man who can do that!"

Philippe noticed he was packing, "Yes, I know. What are you doing?"

"Packing."

"Yes, I can see that! For what – where are you going?"

"Taking Rose away for a while, I think time away from the castle will do her good. We made plans long ago to visit her birth home and her parents' graves, and while we were there to visit Jessie as well, but you know... I still think it will be therapeutic for her to see her old home again."

"And who all is attending this trip?"

"Just the two of us, why do you ask?"

"You know that I can't allow that; you need to take two guards with you for protection! It can be dangerous on the road."

"No guards, they can't be trusted! I want this to be fun for her as she's not herself. How do you think she will feel to be guarded all the time? Exactly like in the castle, no - no guards!" Antoine was thinking of the two guards that killed Jessie.

"I will invite Léo, and I will think of another person."

"Take Ollie. I don't need him now, and I trust him to protect you all. He's a skilled swordsman and knows all the traps if there are any. I will inform him to pack and be ready by tomorrow."

Ollie was surprised by the prince's request and gladly agreed to accompany them and see them safely to their destination. He promised Jessie he would keep Rosaline safe, and he would do everything in his power to keep that promise. He was afraid that she was in trouble and never had the time to discuss why Jessie was so scared and hiding.

The four were off early the following day; Ollie on his steed, with Antoine steering the chariot while Rose sat next to him and Léo at the back, relaxing for the long trip ahead. They stopped halfway to the first inn and had a picnic on the road. They reached their next stop at the inn at sunset, making excellent time.

They were given rooms, and the horses were seen to; they had a quick wash before having a lovely bowl of stew with fresh bread and many glasses of wine during and after supper. They retired early and were off at the crack of dawn. Antoine noticed the spirit returning in Rose – it was a start, and he was pleased with his idea of this trip.

The second day was the same, and on the third, Rose steered the horses straight to Jessie's home, adamant to still sleep there as planned. They found a young boy feeding the animals. Antoine paid him what was promised with a little extra. The boy beamed with pleasure and said he was always available and explained where he lived if they ever needed him again.

Rose walked into Jessie's home and looked around at the familiar place, now full of dust. No time wasted; through tears and heartache, she started to clean up and left the men to their own deeds outside. They erected the two tents and made a fire, feeling content with their surroundings. Ollie slaughtered two chickens and placed them on the fire while Rose made tea for them inside. When the chickens were cooked, they opened a bottle of wine and sat around the fire, eating and drinking. There was not much said during the first night, knowing Rose was missing Jessie. The next day they were going out to see her old home where she grew up.

When they arrived at her childhood home, she went straight to her parent's graves and sat there crying and speaking to them. She told them how much she missed them and how she wished they were alive. She desperately needed them, now more than ever, and broke down in heart-rending tears. The men left her alone to say her goodbyes in private and went to knock on the door.

The owner was surprised to see Prince Antoine on his doorstep, unsure what his visit meant, and welcomed them inside with anticipation. He invited them to stay for breakfast, which they accepted. He knew Ollie; they came to collect the taxes not so long ago with the future King Philippe.

Ollie had no idea this was Rose's birth home, and now knowing this, something was bothering him. He excused himself and stood outside, wondering and looking at the place for the first time with new eyes. It hit him hard when it dawned on him, and Ollie could not believe it! Was it true - was she the girl he brought back? It felt like eons ago! He had to find out somehow and knew asking her now would not be the right time. She was going through so many emotions; he could not think when the right time would be. Ollie thought it best to leave it for now.

Rose returned with her eyes blood-red and said she had to wash up before meeting the new owner. Ollie sneaked her in and went to join the others.

Anthony felt uneasy in his own home, still uncertain why they were here, and no one was explaining. He decided to be straightforward and asked, "Prince Antoine, I am pleased that you came to visit me; however, may I be bold to ask what the purpose of this visit may be?"

"Yes, sorry, my good man, how rude of me! We never actually came to visit you, but this house itself."

This confused Anthony even more; the house was given to him after the previous owners passed away – are they redeciding on the matter? He actually grew attached to the place and was living in luxury. Just then, Rose walked in before Anthony could inquire more about the subject.

"Lady Rosaline Dumont?"

"Anthony! So, you are the new owner." She was not shocked, just surprised that her father's assistant was living in her old home. Most things still looked the same. Certain things were missing, most probably through the raids at the time of the measles; minor changes were made to suit his taste.

"I am so sorry for the loss of your parents, Lady Dumont. They were good decent people!" It was the proper thing to say after not seeing her for so long. He was not surprised that she was with the prince; he had heard of her return and was wondering when she'd make a turn. Has she asked for her home back?

Rose could see Anthony was worried and knew what he might be thinking – she eased his mind. "I just came to see the

105

house again and visit my parent's graves. Thank you for keeping it tidy, and the house is well looked after."

"Thank you, milady. Will you be staying long? I can offer you rooms for the night?"

"No, thank you, we are settled for the time being. Not sure how long we are staying, though, but I might visit again before we leave – if that is alright with you?"

"You are welcome to visit whenever you wish, Lady Dumont."

"Thank you, Sir Anthony!"

The servant walked in to say that breakfast was ready, and she freaked out when she noticed Rose standing there.

"Miss Rosaline! How good it is to see your face again, and may I say you look all grown up." The servant could not help herself and started to cry.

"Alice? I thought the worst of you; how are you and your family?" Rose walked over and hugged her old kitchen servant.

"Oh miss, we are all fine except my oldest daughter, Agnes. Sadly, we lost her too from the plague."

"I'm so sorry, Alice; please send my regards to your husband and the kids."

"I will miss, thank you, miss." Alice straightened up and announced again the food was ready and left. They all enjoyed a hearty breakfast and departed once again to Jessie's place.

*R*ose spent the next day pulling out all the weeds in the vegetable and herb garden. She felt peaceful and at home. When she finished, she watered them and sat down to join the men around the fire. Ollie noticed that Rose was not scared of hard work and respected her more. He saw a different person altogether at this place. She told them of her time when she used to visit here and how Jessie taught her to make some of the mixtures for common incidents and treat them. Rose was her carefree self again and was happy to share this little information with her companions.

Antoine thought he could get a few truthful answers from Rose while they were here, hoping she would share. The four of them were close enough friends to be open with one another. Antoine asked what he thought he knew the answer to.

"Rose, my love, I need to ask you something important, and I need you to be honest with me. Was Jessie my sister – half-sister, that is? Before you answer, remember I said that she reminded me of someone and that maybe I've seen her before?" Rose nodded in answer. "Well, she has all the features of my deceased brother Louis. I thought that perhaps my father had an affair with her mother, and that's why she wanted to hide and not be noticed? Is this true? She must have said something to you?"

Rose knew it was not her place to say, but Jessie was no longer with them and thought she would not mind. Rose was straightforward with her answer.

"Well, she has spoken to me, and yes – she was your half-sister. But not the way you think she was conceived." She did not want to lie to them or give a false statement, even if that meant disrespecting and accusing the king of rape – which was true. Jessie would never lie about a thing like that. Rose took a deep breath and told them precisely what Jessie told her when her mother was here and what happened to her.

When she finished explaining, Antoine stood up and walked toward where the animals were resting. He stared at them, though, not looking. Antoine felt kicked in the teeth for what his father had done to an innocent woman. He could not believe he could hate his father more than he did at this very moment. He ordered his own daughter to be slaughtered on the side of the road without any feelings at all toward his own blood. He could just imagine what his father would do to him if he found out about his personal sex life. He was thankful that Rose told him; with this, he would also share something with her. He did not care anymore and wished his father ill. He went to join them again, and Léo asked if he was all right – he said yes.

"Rose, I have something to tell you too." He looked at Ollie, not knowing what he would do with the information he was about to share with them.

"The day when we left to send Jessie off, there were two guards following us. At first, I thought nothing of it. I thought they were sent to protect us, but they were not seen on our way back, and I put it aside. Until I heard of Jessie's demise, it came back to me, and I realized what happened. You see, they were my father's personal guards, and I believe he ordered to have her killed."

Rose half raised her voice in answer, "What! Are you sure? Have you confronted him about this?"

"No, how can I? But we are sure it was him, and we can't fathom out why he would?"

"Oh, my poor Jessie, she was right to be scared! Your father is an evil man, and I wish nothing good for him!"

"I understand. I feel the same toward him, but I do stress that we should not cross him for fear of what he may do to others or you – even us – who knows?"

"Thus, he gets away with everything he has done?"

"I guess so; he is the king and can order whatever pleases him. Remember that, please."

Ollie just sat listening to everything and could not believe what he was hearing. Poor Jessie and her mother – both were hurt under the king's hands. Worse for Jessie and his own daughter on top of that! To have lived with the thought of how she was conceived – of who she was – even though her mother loved her, it could not have been easy. He felt sorry for Rosaline as well. Ollie could see the pain in her – a lot was troubling Rose. He wanted to enfold her in his arms and keep her safe.

But at this time, he had no idea what to do with this news. He promised Jessie he would avenge her demise, which was impossible to do against the King of France. However, he will do his utmost to keep the other promise - to keep Rosaline safe.

They were silent, and Rose had no appetite. She excused herself after hearing this and went to sleep on Jessie's bed.

Early the following day, they were packing up and were ready to leave, also expecting to make a last turn for Rose to visit her parent's graves - Rose was sitting inside thinking. Léo came in to tell her they were ready to depart. She walked out; Ollie was on his horse, waiting and all set for the journey. Rose announced that she was staying and not returning; this was her home from now on. Antoine was upset to hear this but, in a way, not much surprised. Ollie jumped down from his horse and said he would be staying as well. He was busy removing a tent for his living arrangements.

Antoine said, "Rose, you can't stay here by yourself! You are still a lady - that's going to be like living as a peasant. Are you sure this is what you want?"

"I'm fine with that, Antoine, and happy with my choice. Please don't tell anyone of my location except Philippe. Ollie, I need you to leave with them and protect them until they are home safely. I am fine here and can look after myself. I was taught by a very dear friend of mine how to survive." Thinking of Popi and how much she taught her when she helped in the kitchen to preserve food to last longer. "I also need the clothes I left behind and some personal items. Not my gowns, but my other clothing that's in the drawers. Antoine, could you please pack them for me with my other personal belongings and ask Philippe if Ollie could bring them to me? That's if you don't mind, Ollie?"

"I'll do my best!" Ollie answered.

Antoine said, "With pleasure, and Philippe will not mind. I'm going to miss having you around, my dear friend Rose. When he hugged her, he gave her a bag of coins to see her through until he could send more. They all hugged her and were off once again, leaving Rose behind.

The king heard about this woman that Rosaline was hiding in her room. Her appointed servant, Clara, was upset that she received orders from a peasant person, which she complained about among the other servants. The king's servant was listening and informed King Louis of this new information. He asked Clara to keep an eye on Rosaline since she returned from her captors and listen for any gossip. The king was curious to see who this woman was sharing a room with Lady Dumont, and why were they keeping it a secret? He decided to spy on them so he could see for himself.

His servant informed him that a picnic basket was ordered from the kitchen to be packed for the next day. She also told him that they usually walked out the back through the kitchen whenever they left for their outings. He found a well-hidden spot close to the kitchen – and waited patiently to spy on them.

Rosaline was not accompanying the woman this morning when she exited the kitchen. Louis went ice-cold when he saw her face. What the king saw scared him. He saw the resemblance to his deceased son in her eyes, but why would she bear a likeness to him? The other features were that of an Indian. The only Indian woman he had ever known was a former healer he had many years ago when he was still a young prince. After considering it for a while, he realized she could be his child! She was the result of his actions. He was at a loss – what should he do? He couldn't even think straight when this new light dawned on him.

Thinking back, he did have respect for his healer. She had helped him out a lot during his active, youthful days and not married yet, and the repercussions of his sexual activities. When his father found out about this, he was angry, they argued, and his father forced him to stop his antics. Louis had been very upset about this, that he drank too much on one of his hunting expeditions. When he saw his healer at the same river, he called out to her. Louis had not at first planned his behavior that followed after that. He was sorry the following day once he had sobered up. However, he never saw her again to sort of apologize for his assault – and left it like that.

112

Now that that day's actions were facing him, he felt ashamed for what he had done, and the aftermath was now walking around in his castle. His daughter must have known about this, the reason for her hiding from him and not wanting to show her face in the palace – he wondered who else knew? *Did Rosaline know? Was that why she was helping to hide her?* He did not think so and believed Rosaline to be clueless. He had to stop this woman before she could utter his shame or maybe, perhaps, try facing his daughter to find out for himself. Hoping and wishing, she kept her secret to herself.

If they knew each other well enough to share a room – it must mean they knew each other from Rosaline's days with her parents, and he believed she did not share her secret with them either. He remembered Jacq, Rosaline's father, saying they had a good healer in the village – it must have been her. Her parents showed no difference in their respect or friendship toward him. Why hasn't she faced him or came forward to say who she was – why hide?

Trying to grasp all these questions in his mind was driving him insane. He deliberated carefully about what to do. The only conclusion that came to mind was terminating the bug. He ordered two of his most trusted guards to keep an eye on her and gave orders for her demise. He believed that that would settle his problem and relax his state of mind. They were to take action only when she departed and far from the castle. Rosaline would never know it was him, or could ever guess his actions toward his daughter. They still thought he was in the dark with her presence in the castle and would keep it that way. He was ashamed and believing with her *gone*; he would no longer have those guilty feelings.

Louis was upset that the body returned to the castle. He did not expect this to happen! He was also annoyed with all the chaos it was causing. With an innocent face, he confronted his son to ask what was happening.

6

Var and Popi had told her she was strong and brave – but being and feeling so alone, Rose felt weak and hopeless after losing so much in her life. Why did she have to lose another that was dear to her heart – why could she not keep one alive? Rose was afraid and felt far from brave or strong. Perhaps it was her; that she was the bad seed in the fruit! Perhaps if people stayed away and she made no other friends – or stayed away from her close friends, they would be safe, and her heart would not break further. No – she was losing her mind here, alone all day and with no one to talk to, just the animals and herself – left alone with her depressing thoughts.

Rose was thinking like a Viking now with their superstitious beliefs – that was not like her, and none that happened was her fault! It's life's circumstances that brought her here, and it was up to her alone to make something of her life. Not to blame or give up, but to fight for life – for hope. If she was brave and tough, it was time to be that – try to be. To believe that good things happen and she will be happy again, being here, was just one step towards taking control of her life.

Jessie also believed in her inner strength – it was time to live. Rose took a deep breath, feeling content and calm with her decision. Deciding to stay behind was a good idea, and believed it would all work out in the end.

She picked a few vegetables and some herbs for soup and went inside to wash them before putting the pot on the fire. She took flour out of the cupboard and fetched an egg and goat's milk to bake bread with the soup.

The soup came out nice and thick. Rose was happy with her day's activities. She threw a little more water in the pot for fear that it might burn at the bottom. The soup had to stay on the coals until she ate it all for fear of food spoilage. There was no way to pack cooked food away in this heat. She would have soup for supper, and by the looks of it, for breakfast as well. For the first time since arriving back in her homeland, she felt a sense of calm, and although she was lonely, she also felt peaceful.

While she had her breakfast soup the following day, the young boy that tended to the animals came round to see if anyone was still there.

"Morning misses."

Rose remembered the boy, though she couldn't recall if he had given his name – her mind at the time of arriving at Jessie's place had been elsewhere. Dear Antoine had taken charge of the boy. "Good morning. What may I call you?"

"My name is Jacq."

"Oh... What a blessed and great name you have. That was my father's name as well."

"Really, miss."

"Well, yes, he was a very good man. Are you a good boy?"

Eager to please, "Yes, ma'am, very good."

"I hope so. That name comes only from good people."

"Thank you, miss." Jacq smiled innocently at her.

"Now, why have you come to visit me?"

"Some folks were wondering when Miss Jessie would be back. They require ointments and medications."

Rose was not sure how to inform the young boy of death; still, it looked like he could handle the news. She was also excited and thought maybe she could help – that this was her calling. Popi taught her many things.

"Well, Jacq, I'm sorry to say that Jessie is no longer with us, but maybe I can help with this problem. Let's make a pact, you work for me by hearing what they need, and I will see if I can make it? I was taught very well in the trade." Rose wasn't sure how Jessie's paying arrangements had been with the locals; however, she would allow them to send the payment first and would take it from there. She could make a living off this and was eager to start – to be doing something useful again.

Even the boy was keen to be working again. He agreed and was off to get orders. Jacq would be her connection to the outside world while she was hiding from it. She was content with the idea for now. She went straight to the herb garden, looked at what was there, and then walked around the back to see what was growing in the wild bushes. There was always something hiding and useful. Rose saw non-poisonous mushrooms and other wild herbs.

Jessie's small carriage was parked nicely behind the house and would come in handy when she needs to go to the market for supplies. *'I'd have to try and buy a horse or ask for Jessie's old one to be brought to me,'* she thought. She went back to the herb garden and picked a few herbs to make a simple ointment for sores and bruises, balms they often made during the Viking seasonal celebrations. There was enough to fill four small jars. Even though Jessie was stocked up on empty bottles and jars, she would have to find out where to buy more when she ran out. Jessie left many other herbs hanging around the place that was already dry, which would come in handy when needed.

Rose looked for a writing implement and paper to take down notes. She felt terrible scratching around, but she knew Jessie would not mind and would be pleased with what she was doing. It was her home now. She wanted to write down which herbs were needed for certain illnesses while her mind was still fresh from Popi's lessons.

Later that night, Rose made more fresh bread, scrambled some eggs, and had a cup of tea afterward. She tidied up and started on a new ointment, this time for rashes and itchy bites from insects. She picked the herbs she needed, locked the door behind her, and started humming while she washed them. The ointment came out a little watery, which was still fine, and she filled six small bottles with it.

Jacq came back the next day with seven orders. He said one was for a terrible headache; the other was stomach pain, a nasty cut on the arm, and so on. She wrote everything down and started with the easy ones first – headache – another familiar task they regularly made for the many festivals, and it worked. She would try to make it a little stronger, seeing that it was an awful one. She picked the herbs and once again washed them clean of all soil. Jacq just sat there, not knowing what to do next, he offered to help, but Rose said she was fine for now. Thus, he sat and watched her make the first medication. When Rose finished, she wrote on the bottle, 'headache.'

She saw that Jacq was bored and asked him to feed the animals as he was used to and knew where everything was. Then when he was done, to go around the house and pick her two mushrooms. When she finished the necessary orders, she gave him the bottles and explained what the person with the bad wound had to do. To clean the wound first, then only use the ointment and cover it well. She sent clean bandages in case it was required.

"Remember to inform him to clean it every second day with fresh ointment for a week and then afterward, to leave it open to heal correctly." She wasn't sure how bad the cut was. Jacq just said it was deep. "Stomach pain; three times a day, for two days, then afterward, only when needed. Same for the headaches." She went on to explain the rest. He was a clever boy; he remembered everything when she asked him to repeat what she said.

"Good boy, be careful with the bottles. I'll be waiting for the next orders."

Jacq arrived early the next day, always on time, pulling a small cart behind him with her payments and new orders. She was busy with breakfast and fed him scrambled eggs and a piece of bread first before inspecting what lay waiting in the cart.

There was a bag of flour, cheese, ham, jam, butter, and fat for frying. Rose was pleased with her payments, and at lunch, made them a sandwich with ham and cheese. The boy enjoyed it and was smiling, pleased with the treat.

After the meal, Rose went outside and started digging a hole close to the house where there was constant shade. She placed a sizeable clean rag inside to cover the edges and threw water inside to moisten the hole. Rose wrapped the cheese and the ham further with another damp cloth and placed it inside; she then covered it with a lid that fitted perfectly around the edges so the sand would not fall in. She threw more sand over the top and poured more water over it; she was pleased with her work.

Jacq looked confused. "Miss - why are you burying your food? Don't you want it anymore?" It was the only conclusion he could think of.

120

Rose liked Jacq. She ruffled his hair and laughed, "No, this is how you keep your food cold until the next time you need it, so it does not spoil in the heat, or you have to eat it all at once."

"Does it work?"

"Yes, it does. When I decide to use it again, I will invite you to help me dig it up, and you will see for yourself."

He was very impressed with this beautiful woman and the things she could do.

"May I tell my ma about this so she too can do it?"

Rose laughed again, "Yes, you may, but tell her it must be in a permanent shade where it is always cool and to remember to throw water over at least twice a day, in the morning and the evening."

"I will, miss, thank you!" The boy could not wait to share this with his mother. Jacq gave her four more orders, and she started straight away. He fed the animals and waited to collect the items. The boy went home, pulling his small cart behind him with his cargo on it, and would return fully packed with her payments the next day. He, too, felt he was doing something practical to help others. Rose still had her coins that Antoine gave and rewarded Jacq every week for his dedication and hard work. She was grateful to have him around on her lonely days.

Some mornings, while they enjoyed their breakfast, Rose was curious about the boy's life, and she would ask him questions. Like Rose, Jacq was an only child; his father passed away during the measle plague. His mother has not been well for many years and can't work, so Jacq goes out looking for odd jobs to support her. Though his mother is grateful for her son's care and support, she also tries to make things to sell when she has the energy. Jacq feels blessed to be helping the beautiful lady, and she pays him well. They want for nothing at the time being and is grateful for what they have.

Rose did inquire what was ailing his mother and tries to help where she can; she sends free medication on a weekly basis to help her. Rose even showed Jacq once how to make it. He was intrigued by the lesson.

During their afternoons, while having lunch, she would teach him to read and write as well – he was eager to learn and a fast learner. He also asked many questions about the healing trade and seemed interested to know. Though he was still young, Rose allowed him to watch while she made ointments and medication; she would explain while she was working – Jacq soaked up every lesson.

7

*I*t had been over a month since Antoine and the others left, and Rose wondered when Ollie would return. She was often washing the few garments she had to wear. Every third day, she had a bath in the river that flowed past the cottage; however, she still washed every night after the long dusty, and humid days that passed. Rose badly wanted the clothes that Popi and her daughters made for her. She would feel more relaxed in them. Rose tore pieces off a gown and tried very carefully to sew some pieces together. The result was horrid; she could hear what Sigrid always said with her sewing attempts and laughed at the memory.

The healing trade and the thought of them were the only things that kept her going. That night she decided to make a chicken stew and wanted to invite Jacq to stay for supper for some company, but she did not want him walking back home in the dark. There would definitely be leftovers so she could treat him for breakfast or lunch.

That night in bed, Rose found it difficult to sleep and kept tossing and turning. For the first time, she felt a lump under the mattress and got up to inspect. She found a small notebook and climbed back in bed with it. Inside were Jessie's handwriting and all her notes on potions. What herbs to use for certain potions and how to make them. It would surely come in handy and help her a great deal, and she was thankful for the finding. Rose set it aside and tried again to sleep.

Not long, she heard a noise outside and was petrified and wondered who would be crawling around her house at this time of night. She picked up a knife and walked silently to the door. A loud knock came, which made her jump out of her skin.

"Who is there?" she called out in a shaky voice.

"It's me, Ollie, Lady Dumont."

Rose was relieved to hear his voice rather than some intruder. She was so happy to see him that she hugged him in greeting when she opened the door.

She invited him inside and offered him some chicken stew; he complimented her cooking and had two helpings. She was pleased he enjoyed it. Ollie explained why he took so long to return. Rose smiled and said that it was no problem; she was just glad he was back. He asked how she was coping, and she told him what she was up to and about her new friend that was helping.

He stood up and brought her packages inside and more money from Philippe. Rose was appreciative of their generosity. They both sat in silence for a while, unsure what to say next; Rose felt exhausted and gave a huge yawn.

Ollie smiled, stood up once again, and said good night, "Will see you in the morning." He went outside to set up his tent and made a fire.

Rose made breakfast for them and left some for Jacq when he arrives. She felt more comfortable with her Viking clothes to do the necessary chores inside and outside the house. Rose was feeling chipper again in her situation.

Ollie wondered who gave her those clothes or where she got them. It reminded him of his roots.

"How long can you stay?" Rose asked him.

"As long as you need me, milady, or when I'm sent for. I asked them to send a message to Sir Anthony's place, and I'll make a turn there occasionally to see if any arrived."

"Please call me Rose. It feels weird been called a lady or anything in my situation at the moment; after all, we are friends, are we not?" She said this while smiling sweetly.

"Indeed, we are friends, and very well – Rose," and returned her smile.

Rose was glad to have a grown-up around to have an adult conversation with again, but why were they so uneasy being alone together? He still reminded her of Thord a lot, and that bothered her. The kiss they shared outside the kitchen once when she was a little intoxicated was very passionate. Not like

125

Thord used to kiss her – his kisses were gentle and slow but also intense. The two men were so different from each other.

They got along well for their first week together, secret glances and feelings growing, which both parties could not fathom out yet. On the day he was visiting Anthony's house to hear if any letters arrived for him, he invited her to join him on his travels. Rose gladly accepted, needing a break from her duties; she made enough potions that were in general need to take a day off. Also, as she was wearing the clothes that Sigrid, Popi's daughter, gave her, she had to dress decently again as a lady should in public.

Ollie did not think of bringing another horse for her; therefore, they had to share. Their bodies touching and closeness gave both an electric feeling; Rose blushed, not from being shy, but with his touch alone; it gave her a warm feeling inside. They did not speak much on this short trip, so she tried to clear her mind on her duties thus far.

To her surprise, a letter arrived for her as well; it was from Antoine. Rose would not open it until she got home. They came just in time for lunch, and Anthony invited them to stay; it was something different from her daily cooking, and they enjoyed the treat.

After lunch and relaxing in the parlor with warm drinks, Anthony said, "Since last you were here, I was waiting for your return Lady Dumont. There is something that I kept and packed away until I saw you again. Not sure if or when – after all the stories that went around, but I'm glad you came home safely." He left to fetch her package; Rose was not sure what it could be. He walked in with a huge box and placed it on the table in front of her. "You can open it whenever it pleases you. That is all I found after I moved in. The villagers badly raided the house at that time."

Curiosity got the better of her, and she opened the box. Inside were some of her mother's trinkets and personal belongings. She slowly went through them; tears ran down her cheeks, remembering her mother wearing each and every item. There were a few of her own personal belongings and things her parents gave her on special days.

"Thank you so much for this, Anthony! I can't thank you enough for keeping this for me. You have no idea what your kindness of putting this aside means to me."

He hesitated before he spoke again, "You are more than welcome to take anything else in the house. This was your home; you grew up here, and everything belongs to you."

Rose looked around the parlor, thought of all the fancy furniture in the house, and smiled. "Thank you for the offer Sir Anthony, but they are all just material things, and I'm in no need of them. I am content with what I have and my living arrangements at the moment." She looked at the box he gave a few minutes ago and touched it. "This will do just fine, thank you." She couldn't imagine a fancy chair in Jessie's home or anything else that would fit in there and wanted to laugh at the image in her head.

"I'm glad you are happy. Something else arrived with your letter – a horse. It is in the stables waiting for you to claim it – two, actually."

"Oh?" Rose touched the letter and could not wait to read it.

"Prince Antoine is a dear and a kind friend. I shall have to thank him as soon as I can send a letter."

"You may bring your letters to me, and I'll make sure he receives them."

"Thank you so much. You are too kind."

They sent a healthy, sturdy horse for her with Jessie's old steed. Thinking she would want it as well. She was happy to see the old mount again and knew how much it meant to Jessie. She would always care for it.

Rose waited until she was in bed to read the letter from Antoine, it was long, and it made her laugh; she missed him *so* much. The horse was from Philippe; he said it was a gift and couldn't be returned! Rose was not complaining, a horse was sorely needed, and it was a beauty. That's what she'll name her; Beauty.

Rose felt safe with Ollie around, and their friendship grew as each day went by, as Antoine may have guessed. In the letter, he said that Ollie was a good and trusted friend, and she could not go wrong with such a handsome steed without trying to tame him. That was so unexpected that she rolled with laughter. Calling a man a steed was so Antoine. She could not sleep and peeped outside to see if Ollie was sleeping. He was looking up at the night sky, daydreaming.

"Penny for your thoughts," Rose smiled.

"If you make it four pennies, I'll consider it!" he answered, and she laughed. "I could hear you were enjoying your letter?"

"Yes, I do so miss talking to him; he could always make me laugh. I wonder why he has never taken a partner yet? All the women are fond of him."

Ollie thought she knew because they were so close. "I assumed you knew?"

"Knew what?"

"About Antoine's choice in a partner?"

"What are you talking about?" *Choice in a partner – it made no sense.*

"Well, Rose, I'm sorry to inform you; your best friend prefers the same sex as him!" Ollie looked at Rose, and her eyes grew big.

"Léo?"

"Yes!"

Rose placed her hands over her mouth in disbelief. "Oh, my... how did I miss that one!" They both burst out into laughter. "Well, good for him, whatever makes him happy. Who knows this secret?"

Ollie explained, "I'm not sure. I was not supposed to know, except I caught them one evening on our way back to the castle when we left here. We were camping outside; Antoine's idea, he was not in the mood for a tavern or any noise. I killed the fire first before warning them about bandits passing and to be quiet. They were terrified; I assured them that their secret was safe with me. However, I do believe Philippe knows as well. I can't say how, but it's a feeling. You know the king ordered Antoine to marry you, and he refused. Not that he would if he could, but Antoine knows he could never make you happy as a marriage partner or give you what a husband should."

"No, I did not know. Why has he not shared this with me?"

"Many things are going on in your life. It seemed insignificant at the time. We spoke a lot on the road, and he opened up about many things."

Rose thought about what he had said in the letter. 'He can be trusted, and he's a good friend.' *I do so love him,* she thought, *the king will force a marriage on him one day, and that will not work. The king must never know of this secret. Who knows what he'll do to Antoine!* Rose was worried for her friend and prayed that Antoine and Léo were careful not to show their affections in company.

Ollie tried to find out a little more about Rose on their trip. However, Antoine would not budge. He said that Ollie would have to ask himself about what happened to her or where she was. He thought that Ollie and Rose were a perfect match, and them spending quality time together will surely awaken the beast. Rose was eighteen, and he guessed Ollie was around twenty-five or twenty-six – still young enough to marry and start over. He didn't believe there was an age limit to start over with another - they were both still young to start a family.

"Where have you learned these skills to survive the way you do - and who taught you to make potions? You said Jessie taught you the basics, but from what I'm seeing, you are a skilled healer."

"Well, thank you, Sir Waters." They had opened a bottle of wine earlier and were enjoying it in each other's company.

"If I told you, I would have to kill you. Are you willing to die for this information?" The wine was already working through her system, and Rose was in a playful mood.

"I can't be certain, but I know I wish to live, so it's all up to you?" He smiled, enjoying this side of her.

"Well, it's actually a long story, and coming back recently, I heard more than I wished to know. So... Where do I start...?"

"From the beginning, I presume."

"Well, let's see... I was just... No! You should hear my side to know what all this means to me; then maybe you can tell me what I should do? I will not start with what Jessie told me. That would be too easy." Rose smiled and offered her glass to be filled. It reminded her of the time they told stories around the fire after dinner with the Vikings. Popi's husband, Var, could tell a good story!

"Now, it was a terrible time in these parts of the land, and many people were dying." She laughed at her own beginning, and he chuckled as well. "I was hidden well behind a huge rock by Jessie to be fetched later again to leave this place, but when Jessie returned, I was gone...!"

Ollie abruptly stood up and showed her to be quiet – he heard something moving in the bushes. He ushered her quickly into the house and closed the door while he went to inspect the noise.

While he was gone, she made herself a cup of tea to sober up. It took a while before he returned, and when he came in, he said someone needed to see her. Rose could not fathom out who would visit her at this hour. It was very late! Antoine would have said something in his letter. Maybe it was a villager who needed urgent medication. Ollie reassured her that it was safe and she should meet her guest. When Rose stepped out, she noticed a short old Indian woman staring at her. She was not sure who this was and just stared back.

Ollie stood behind Rose and told her it was Jessie's mother. Rose's mind sobered instantly and could see some resemblance; she had heard so much about her, and now facing Jessie's mother for the first time, it had a tremendous emotional impact on her; she could at first not find the words. Jessie had shown her once how to greet an Indian if ever you came across one. Rose walked over to the older woman and greeted her. The woman greeted back with a smile. She was close to tears but forced them back. Rose invited her inside, but the woman declined and pointed towards the fire, preferring to sit outside.

The three sat in silence for a while; no one knew what to say, so Ollie started the conversation. "Wise old woman of the earth, why have you traveled so far?"

She looked at Rose. "My daughter knew you. She sees you as family. You are the Rose she loves? She sent me many messages over the years during her absence."

Rose was touched. "Yes, I am."

"I know something is wrong, I felt it, and I traveled this far to find out."

Rose looked to Ollie for guidance. He told her to be herself and to be honest.

"I am so sorry to tell you this; she has passed on to another life," Rose had to wipe a tear away; the pain was still fresh, and voicing it to Jessie's mother made it worse. Rose explained what she had done for Jessie at her funeral.

The old woman was touched that Rose would go through all that and follow their tradition for her daughter. She asked if she could spend the night and give her personal send-off at Jessie's home. Ollie offered her his tent; they left her to perform her own custom of sending a spirit off and saying goodbye to her only daughter. They watched in the beginning, standing in the doorway of the cottage.

The old woman threw more wood in the fire – the flames were huge and wild. She then painted her face red. She slowly started dancing around the fire speaking in her native tongue. Then the dance intensified, and the words became louder;

when she began to moan, Rose closed the door and cried for the pain the poor woman was going through.

Ollie was consoling Rose. He, too, felt their pain. The wailing was so loud they could hear the pain through her words. It was something they both experienced for the first time and would never want a repeat. Ollie had his bedroll and placed it close to the fireplace. He let Rose sleep – with the wine and this new arrival, she was exhausted.

The following day, Jessie's mother was gone! It was as if she had never been there. Rose went about her daily chores to take her mind off the previous night. Jacq came early and said that the man that had the cut, in the beginning, was complaining about the pain. He said the man's arm was not healing correctly and asked if Rose could see him. She needed this distraction, so she packed clean bandages and a sterile wound liquid she made with potent ointment and needle and thread just in case. Ollie would not let her go alone; thus, he joined them on their mission.

The man's arm was infected – the pus was oozing out of it. Rose took out a small knife and asked Ollie to sharpen it on the stone she offered – it needed to be a clean and easy cut; she did not want to inflict unnecessary pain. He was already suffering. Rose took a clean rag and tried to squeeze some of the pus out – the smell was awful!

When she was happy with step one, she took her knife from Ollie and sterilized it before reopening the wound. Thanks to Ollie, the knife was perfectly sharp and cut easily – the man did not even flinch. She reopened the wound, and more pus and old blood came pouring out. Rose let it flow for a few minutes, making sure it was clean – then threw some of the wound cleaner over the opening – she did this a few times before taking the next step. The man was in pain but put on a brave face.

Rose took the thread out and laid it in the wound cleaning liquid while she sterilized the needle. She always hated this part of the exercises that Popi gave them. Although Rose knew how to suture an injury, she always let Sigrid do the stitching. Popi had them practice on a pigskin. Rose could not sew material together, but Popi was always impressed with how she stitched a gash, so Rose knew she could do this.

She pulled the thread through the needle and looked at the man, and he nodded. Rose pulled the skin towards each other and pulled the first stitch through, *so far so good*, she thought. With each stitch, it became more manageable, and in no time, she was done.

Rose cleaned it further, rubbed some ointment on, and bandaged it. She told the man, "You can't do any hard labor or use your arm for a while because the stitches will reopen."

The man looked troubled, "Miss, I can't promise. I need to work and can't skip a day because I need to feed my family." Rose looked at Ollie; she didn't know what to do. Not expecting his generosity, Ollie took a few coins out of his pocket and gave them to the man. The man thanked him profusely for his kindness.

Rose left ointment behind and some medication to last a few days for him to sleep the pain away. She promised to visit again in a week to inspect the wound. He was thankful for her help and grateful for the money to feed his family while he was incapable of supporting them.

That week went smoothly; everyone had their own activities to keep them busy. Rose and Jacq never skipped a day with his reading and writing lessons, while Ollie helped around the house fixing things. Jacq would drop off her payment parcels and return home with his new medication orders. Whenever he brought the payments of something nice to eat, Rose would make lunch for them all, and afterward, Jacq would help place the rest in the cooling hole with Rose.

Once, they got paid with a nice thick steak and some bacon. Rose was so happy she hugged Jacq, and occasionally, when he left in the late afternoon, she would kiss him on the cheek to thank him for all his hard and honest labor.

"I think he has a crush on you."

Rose was busy pulling the weeds out before taking what she needed for supper.

"What, Jacq? Don't be silly! I'm much older than he is, and he's just a boy."

"That's how a crush starts. Jacq looks up to you and respects you. You are a beautiful woman - person. You must see the way he eyes me as if to say; I'm not wanted or needed here."

"You're silly, and even so, I think it's sweet. Jacq's a good child, and now I have two protectors." She smiled at Ollie and flushed with the compliment. Rose stood, and before entering the cottage, not turning to face him, she said, "Thank you!" then walked inside.

Rose became more familiar with Ollie; spending each day together made her realize what kind of person he truly was, kind and generous. When he should leave, Rose knew his presence would certainly be missed - she every so often loved to watch him work. Ollie was incredibly handsome and sturdy.

Their first kiss kept lingering in her mind, and every so often, he would catch her staring, with her immediately looking the other way. She felt uncomfortable for even having such thoughts. Rose attempted to stay busy, trying hard not to ponder on this intimate subject.

Ollie was not innocent either in this situation, sometimes he could not take his eyes off her, and he did not hide the fact. He had to constantly apply self-control, especially during the evenings around the campfire, which he had to restrain himself from grabbing and kissing her.

8

$\mathcal{A}$ week later, as promised, Rose made a call on the man with the stitches. It was looking much better. She told him to leave it open and keep it clean at all times to prevent infection again. She promised to return after a week to remove the stitches. After their rounds to the sick, they made a turn at Anthony's house. Only Ollie went in while Rose attended her parents' graves.

There were no messages for them, and they kindly declined the offer for lunch on this day. If they had stayed for lunch as they usually did, they would have received one. The messenger was not far from the Village, and Anthony had not been able to send it anywhere, not knowing where they were staying.

They had not told him, and it never occurred to him or bothered to acquire the information regarding their lodging. However, like clockwork, they returned every week. The letter had to wait a week before they could read its contents. The messenger, at the time of delivery, had not said that it was of utmost importance.

Ollie noticed that Rose was more open about herself when she had a few glasses of wine. Not that he wanted to disrespect her; there was still much he wanted to know about Rose and where she had been for over a year. Ollie wanted answers before Philippe ordered him back for duties.

Rose was kneading dough for fresh bread and left it to rise. She was in the mood for fish today, and they made plans to sit by the river and catch a few. As planned, after they caught enough fish, Ollie would clean it and place them on the grill; then, she would bake the bread inside.

While they were relaxing and waiting for the fish to bite, they had a surprise visitor - Jessie's mother returned and was cheerful. They were all happy to see each other, and Rose wondered where she had been.

They invited her to stay for dinner, and Ollie offered his tent once again. The old woman nodded and helped herself in the vegetable garden and went inside to make something. They let her be; she felt comfortable enough around the place and soon returned to join them - smiling. She seemed more relaxed than last time, and Rose was happy to see that. The woman accepted a glass of wine and just listened to the two talking. They eventually asked her where she disappeared to.

"I had to settle something with an old friend I left behind many moons ago," she replied. They accepted her answer.

Ollie caught enough fish and then some. Rose thought she could preserve the rest as pickled fish as she was taught to do.

139

The fish was grilled to perfection. Jessie's mother made a garlic and lemon herb sauce to go with everything; they dipped their bread in it and finished the whole lot! Rose couldn't help to ask for the recipe, and the woman did with pleasure.

They retired after they noticed the older woman yawning and said good night.

Rose and Ollie were wide-awake. He had his bedroll out on the floor close to the fire once again. When they passed each other in that tiny place – he could not fight the urge anymore. Since arriving and spending each day together, he kept thinking of their first kiss and how badly he wanted a repeat – he grabbed Rose around the waist and pulled her close to him; Ollie stared at her with a smile, being sure of his actions.

Rose was thrilled to feel his touch once again and looked up with admiration and returned his smile; that's when he bent down and kissed her with passion. She responded with delight and had been waiting for a rerun since their first time. It went on for a long while until she pulled away for a breather, smiling with pleasure. He was still holding her and smiling down. He started kissing her neck, cheek, and lips and gently kissed her again with more hunger. She was tempted to lose her innocence with this man this very night but knew better.

She stopped him again; she loved the feeling of being in his arms and the way he held onto her; the feeling of being so close was too much too soon to handle. Rose wanted Ollie never to let go. They were still standing and staring at each other, both smiling like two naughty kids. Ollie thought that he would never experience this feeling again after losing his wife; this time around, it was more intense than his first love. The want and need were powerful, and he wondered how he could ever leave Rose alone again when Prince Philippe should call on him.

He kissed her again and never wanted to stop. The taste of her breath was so sweet and so willing, which made it harder to respect her virtue. They sat on her bed because there were only two hard chairs in the cottage, and he still wanted to hold her as much as she allowed him. He would never force himself on her or expect anything more than just kissing and the need to feel close – Rose could not respect him more.

The bed was too small for them both to lie on, so he invited her to share his bedroll on the floor. She was in his arms, kissing and speaking until Rose was exhausted and slept in his arms. He stared at her for a long time, Ollie could not believe his good luck that he found such an amazing woman, and the feeling was mutual.

As soon as he could, he would speak to Philippe about courting her and asking for her hand. Ollie was confident he would approve and give his blessings. He gently moved her hair away from her face, and she gave a slight moan – with that, he pushed her closer and never wanted to let go. Ollie could hardly sleep that night, staring at her innocent face. He knew he loved her with all his heart – from the first moment they met in the meadows.

"Good morning, my flower!" Ollie could not resist and kissed her again. Rose was over the moon to wake up in this man's arms and still be kissed with affection.

"Good morning, Ollie." She blushed and stood up to put a pot on for tea. While he was rolling up his bedroll, she opened the door and was surprised to find the older woman was still there. They all drank their tea outside, and Rose got busy making breakfast.

Jessie's mother never waited for an invite to help; she helped Rose with everything. Jacq arrived just in time to join them. He later gave more orders, and when Jessie's mother realized what Rose was doing, she was amazed. She helped with the preparation, and they were finished in no time. She said her goodbyes after lunch. Rose gave Jessie's old steed for her to take home. It just felt right that it should return with her.

The woman held both of Rose's hands and said, "My Jessie said these words to me when she left home, and I will repeat them to you. You are a good spirit, and I see why my Jessie stayed and never returned."

I give you these words from my heart -
I will always be with you - I will not depart.
I am in the wind that gives you those chills,
I am the sunlight that shines upon you,
On a rainy day, I am in every raindrop that falls,
that gives kisses upon your skin.
When you feel you miss me, look up,

I am in the birds that sing and fly in the sky.
At night, I am the stars that shine and give you light
and the moon that protects you in the dark.
Do not think of me as gone – I will never leave you
and always be with you.

Rose was crying by the time the older woman had finished her poem. Jessie's poem had two meanings; one – if someone missed another and if someone passed away. What a beautiful message.

The woman kissed Rose's hands and went on speaking, "My home is always open to you; you say to those that are my kind that '*Ojinjintka*' which means 'Wildrose' that is you, is seeking for *Paytah* 'fire' this is my name. You will be safe." Rose was blessed with an Indian name and was touched by the invite to visit *Paytah's* people.

"Thank you so much, *Paytah*. I bless and wish you a safe trip home and hope to see you again in the future." Rose wondered and asked, "What does Jessie's name mean?" She was curious to know.

The woman smiled and said, "Gift." Then *Paytah* led her horse through the forest and was gone.

Rose watched in silence as Jessie's mother walked away. After all, she'd been through, it was true how much she loved her daughter and never looked at her differently because of the way she was conceived – Jessie was her mother's 'gift,' and she loved her daughter with her whole soul.

143

Rose looked at Ollie and smiled. "I am an '*Ojinjintka*' –I love it!"

"It suits you as well – my Wildrose." He walked over to hold her and kissed her out in the open. Rose liked the way he said her new name and laughed. "What does your name mean - do you know?"

He was still holding onto her and said, "Ollie? It's not my real name. It was given to me by my comrades and friends. It's a nickname. My real name means of greatness, the ruler of all gods."

"Oh?" Rose teased him. Smiling up to his beautiful face with her arms around his waist, and said, "Oh, great one, please give your true name so I can call upon you when in need." Rose laughed.

"It's Orinn."

Rose froze in his arms, feeling faint, and slowly pulled away from him. She was remembering a story Popi told her - could it be?

With disbelieve and shock in her voice, she asked, "What – what did you say?"

Not knowing what was happening, he repeated his name. "Orinn. Why - what's wrong, Rose?"

"Orinn Waters?" Rose knew none of the Vikings had any last names. "Who gave you the surname?" It was the most unusual thing to ask any person, and he laughed.

"My family! What's wrong with you?"

She was stunned and said, "I thought you were dead! Or so it was told to me." She was thinking back to the story Popi told her of the chief's firstborn and that he was gone - gone! Not dead! She took it all wrong, and once again, she fell for the wrong man. He is a Viking and the chief's son. If he goes home, he will be in line to be chief. Not if, but when - he had to go back - his family needs him!

"Rose, snap out of it! What's got into you?"

She looked at him and asked him to sit down. It was time she explained about her journey - taken by the Vikings, his clan, before returning to the castle. However, she must watch what she says; it's not her place to give any personal information about his losses. He should return home to find out for himself.

Rose was going to be honest and straightforward with him. The shock was still strong, and now she knew why he reminded her of Thord - they were brothers!

"I was taken and saved by Vikings; your tribe. They healed me, your Aunt Popi took great care of me, and they became my family. I had amnesia and could only leave when my memory returned to say where I belonged. I came to love everyone on that island and was sad to leave. To be honest, I wanted to stay but could not. That information I can't share with you because it is not my place to tell you. I see now they were right; it was a good thing to come back and have closure." She paused before her next words. "Your family needs you and misses you terribly."

145

"Wait! Who told you about me?"

"Your Aunt Popi, she misses you very much and never forgot you."

"What did she say?"

"Not much. I just remember your name Orinn; your father named you after his favorite god Odin." Rose could not say that his mother passed not so long afterward. He would be devastated, and it wasn't her place to tell him.

"Just help me with this information. So, you were saved by my tribe and lived with them for over a year, and because I'm the lost son, you want nothing to do with me anymore – am I correct?" Ollie looked dejected and confused.

"No, I do, but I can't! When you go back, you will be chief, and I'm not a Viking."

"My life as a Viking stopped when I left that island! Why can't Thord become chief? Why should I give up everything I have here to go back there? I have responsibilities here now and people that need me more."

"Oh, Orinn, I wish I can tell you, but I can't! You must go back, if not for good, but as I have done for closure. Just see your people again, and if you feel the need to leave, then do so."

"And how will I get there, clever lady?" He was irritated by this time and annoyed with her.

Rose thought about it and realized Olaf and Var were making a stopover before their voyage back home. When they first dropped her off, she was devastated, so much so that she could not stop crying. The thought of them being the last people she would ever see again, her final goodbyes, had been shattering to her soul. That's when they promised to call on her again; Var said they would send someone and will wait for her at a specific location to meet one last time. At the moment, they were still trading outland. She shared this information with Ollie.

"Olaf and Uncle Var!" He would not admit it to her, but the thought of seeing those two soon thrilled him. Olaf had been his best friend before he left. All those years lost on a friendship that could have grown in immense admiration. He wondered how they looked after all these years.

Rose went in to fetch a bottle of wine; they both needed to unwind after the shock.

Ollie was a little nervous thinking about going back. He had thought about seeing his family again; however, he never imagined staying and accepting his destiny of becoming chief – just a visit! Although the Viking blood and some traditions were still in him, he was no longer the same person. His life had changed outside that bubble on the island.

He refilled their glasses and asked, "So, how is my family doing?"

"They are fine, is all I can say. Everyone is fine!"

"You are not going to say much, are you?"

"No! As I said, it's for you to find out for yourself."

"Someone died; that's why you're not speaking much – who is it?"

"Really, Ollie! Can't you just accept the fact that I can't tell you anything since it's not my place to say! Perhaps Var and Olaf can tell you when they arrive. I believe they will when they see you again."

Ollie asked, "If they are returning to say their final greetings, how will you know by hiding in this place? How will they find you?"

Rose had not thought of that, which meant she would have to return to the castle for a while.

Ollie looked at her and wondered, "Are you in love with my brother, Thord?"

"Yes, I was." Rose wanted to be honest with him as much as she can.

"Were the two of you an item – is that why you want these feelings that's growing between us to stop?"

"No, we were not an item. Thord would not allow it to go any further. We were infatuated with each other, but that was it. I think or so believe, more on my side. He strongly valued your father and his wishes to obey the Viking rules, and I respected him for that. I was an outsider."

"My heavens, nothing changed there!" Ollie was furious that Rose felt like an outsider and not welcomed as a human being.

"Don't get me wrong, Orinn. I was treated with kindness and much loved by Popi and her family. We are family; I came to love and learn and accept the Viking rules. They have changed or are starting to grow with the new changes. Many people have stretched their homes further out for more rooms,

148

and that's just a small example. You will see, it's great there, and the freedom to roam around and be yourself is the thing I miss most. I miss the person I became there and miss my family a lot!"

He said nothing and sat watching the flames flickering. He added more logs on the fire and poured wine for them both.

"Rose, my feelings for you are still new, but I know they are strong, and I never want to give that up, even if it means never going back. If I can have you by my side, that is, if you feel the same, then I'll try to think about it. Still, I will not choose one. I will not lose you now – you come first!"

Rose was delighted with those words. That's all she ever wanted in a relationship; to be desired and loved as her parents had each other. She can see them share that kind of love. However, it's an obstacle that he alone has to take and face. She would respect his choice and understand. After Ollie finds out about his losses, she had a feeling that he would not deny his destiny, and Rose was not part of that. The thought of going back and living with Popi again, even if it meant to see him every day and not be able to have him, she would take that risk – or thought she could. She no longer belonged here and so desired to return.

"I will go with you if that is alright with everyone involved, and I will be by your side all the way if you wish, but I really would like to stay there for good if the chief agrees. Oh, Orinn, I don't belong here anymore. I have nothing really, except Jessie's home and being a healer. I love it, but I want more in

149

life than just this. My soul feels lost and floating above me in the clouds waiting for something exciting to happen, to feel alive again. I'm living day to day, not knowing where I'm going or belong.

"The life I had over there with your tribe was unbelievable. You were always working for a goal, and the people are all family. They care and love one another. It was exciting living with them and helping Popi with medication; I learned more there than anyone can learn anywhere. The Vikings that I got to know and love are gentle people, and I love them for that."

Ollie listened to what Rose had to say, and somehow, he understood how she felt.

"What about love and marriage and kids someday - don't you want that too?"

Rose exhaled, "Yes, I do! I want to be loved and give love in return. I want a family; I just don't know how at this moment?"

"Take me, Rose. I am offering you my hand in marriage. I will speak to Philippe, and I think he will approve, then we can go from there."

"Oh, Ollie," Rose was touched with the proposal, and if it were at a different circumstance, she would have definitely said yes. In a soft, sad voice, she answered, "I do wish I can answer you now, but I can't. Let's take this journey together and see what happens."

The conversation went dead. When she got up to say goodnight, he kissed her with all the passion he was feeling. She returned it just the same and went inside. Rose felt that she had lost everything once again. She felt miserable; she was in tears and had a restless night with hardly any sleep. The thought of seeing Popi again and being on that island was exhilarating. She was feeling happy and sad at the same time, giving up on true love to make others happy. They needed some hope on that island. Kiti, the chief's daughter, made her intentions clear she would not marry soon. Therefore, no Chief will be nominated, and his actual son, the chief's blood, should take that honor.

9

The tension between them was slightly different from that night. Ollie wanted to discuss more on the subject of them courting but had a feeling Rose made up her mind about him returning home first. They had a dull week that passed with not many words spoken between them. The scheduled outing occupied their thoughts, and they were getting ready to leave earlier as planned.

After Rose finished removing the man's stitches, she told him that all looked well and that he could return to work again, then they went straight to Anthony's house to see if any letters had arrived. There was one for each of them; hers from Antoine and his from Philippe. Orinn decided to open his as he always did, wanting to know ahead what was asked of him, where Rose liked to read hers in private and alone.

He first read it silently, after which he read it aloud.

My friend Ollie,
I am sad to report that my father, our king, has fallen
ill, and no one knows what's wrong with him. We can't

find a healer, and the priests are doing a terrible job.
Please see if you can find a healer and bring her or him as
soon as you can. It will be much appreciated. We are in
great need of your help. I will be waiting for your arrival.
Please send my regards to Lady Dumont and tell her I
wish her well. I will visit her soon after all this chaos is
over at the castle.

Kind Regards
Prince Philippe

"When did this letter arrive, Sir Anthony?" Orinn stressed.

"A week ago, just after you left, you left no address where you could be found; therefore, it simply had to wait." Anthony looked worried.

Ollie said, "It's fine! Sorry, we can't stay and need to leave straight away."

On their way to Jessie's home, he asked Rose, "Are you up to saving the king? I know how you feel about him, and believe me, the feeling is mutual; still, he is their father, we should try to help where we can."

Rose was not fond of the king; however, she could not refuse to try and help her friends in need. She just nodded and prepared for the trip when they arrived at the cottage. They left as soon as they were packed, which was not much, both on horseback, which would make the trip faster and not necessary to stop at every inn on route to the castle - only one tavern, to rest their horses and themselves and have a meal.

Upon their arrival at the castle, Rose first ordered a bath and donned the attire befitting a lady of the court; she could not be in proper company the way she looked. Her chambers were untouched and were the same as when she left. All her gowns were still hanging in the closet where she left them and was thankful for that – probably under Antoine and Philippe's orders. After a change in appearance, looking like a lady again, she went down to greet her friends. In the king's courters, she found four priests praying and bleeding the king out; he looked terrible. They were so foolish, but she said nothing.

Philippe and Antoine were there waiting for the inevitable to happen with no hope in their eyes. Rose had no idea what to do or how to help; the king looked pale, obviously from losing too much blood. She noticed the bucket next to his bed and caught the sour whiff of vomit, which made her consider the possibility of poison. She was confused with this knowledge that the king was poisoned; she could be wrong as well. How would someone get past his guards to poison the king – and who? If she was right, what kind of poison was another matter. Rose stepped out of the room for a breather – the air inside was stifling because no one bothered to open any windows.

She was so annoyed with the priests for being so idiotic, not believing in the healing power of the herbs created by the same God they were praying to. They believed only in prayer, which made no sense. How was she supposed to help the king? They might accuse her of being a witch! It wouldn't be the first time;

women cannot and are not allowed to have these powers, as they so call them, to heal.

Antoine came out and hugged her.

"I'm so sorry, Antoine; I can try to help, except I can't think how? How did this all happen – when did it start?"

"Thank you for coming, Rose, and may I say it's wonderful to see you again, even under such dire circumstances. It started about a week ago or a little more. It seems no one can help; it's gotten worse with each passing day; he seems to be on his last. Sadly, it may happen soon."

"I'm so sorry! Perhaps if we came sooner, I could have helped?"

"Don't beat yourself up about it; I believe it's his time, and we should accept it." Antoine seemed a little cold towards his father's situation, and she knew why. Nevertheless, he did look sad.

Philippe came out looking downhearted and hugged her.

"Good to see you again, Rosaline; I'm so happy you're here." He looked at Antoine and shook his head. Their father was gone! "I will make the announcement as soon as I can get everyone together in the castle. We will discuss the funeral arrangements as soon as the priests finish cleaning up inside and washing father. He will be left on his bed for anyone who wishes to say their goodbyes before he's taken away." Philippe was not in the mood for any company right now and had work to do as well. With his father the king passing, his new responsibilities put him under a heavy strain. With his shoulders hanging heavy, and before excusing himself, he said, "I will see you all later; I will be occupied for a while. I need to write a few copied letters and send a messenger to post them in each town proclaiming the news."

They both looked sad; no matter what they thought of him or what kind of man he was, he was still their father. The following day everyone wore black in the castle, as was the tradition, until after his funeral, where they could wear their formal clothes again, except for the family.

Rose left Jacq in charge of Jessie's house, so she had no worries on that side. While she was back at the castle, she had more time to think. Rose spent her afternoons with Léo and Antoine and was alone in the evenings. At Jessie's place, she was used to having Ollie around; now, being back at the castle and him being occupied with Philippe all the time, she actually missed him.

They had not spoken about the Viking situation again after that evening. Rose had spent her days cooking and cleaning, then in the gardens and making potions or ointments for her customers. Orinn had not said much either; he felt miserable after being rejected by Rose. His mind had been on his family for the first time in many years.

Philippe made a turn at Rose's chambers one evening, asking, "May we speak? Much is happening now that I have no time for myself anymore."

"Yes, of course, come in." Rose poured them tea, sat down, and waited for him to speak.

"My coronation is soon, and my nerves are at an end. I knew this day would come, but with my father still alive and handling all matters, I was content to wait and help him on the side whenever he allowed me to. He never really let me in on most meetings, thinking he had all the time in the world to rule. He was happy to leave me in charge of the army units, especially now that the war is on again and England will be attacking soon. Our spies still have to return with news on England's movements. I have more than I can handle." Philippe looked tired and had bags under his eyes. "Then it's this topic of marriage that everyone thinks is so important! I have to marry to seek help for the battle ahead. I hear we need more men."

Rose felt sorry for him and tried to give him confidence in himself and his destiny.

"You will be just fine. I promise you that! You are a good man, and you know how to handle yourself in sticky situations. We are all here to help and support you, and you know Antoine will never let you down; you can count on him for anything and trust him more than any adviser. Just remember that!

"Furthermore – I'm always here if you need someone to talk to, for the time being, at least. I was waiting for the right time to tell you that I would be leaving soon. I don't know when or for how long, but I'm going back to the Vikings again." She waited for a reply while he comprehended what she said.

157

"Going back? But why - are you not happy here?" Antoine confided in him about how Jessie was conceived. Philippe was shocked by the news and couldn't be more disgusted by his father. He felt guilty about his father's conduct and thought that was the reason she wanted to leave again. But his father was gone now and thought Rose might move back into the castle. With guilt and sorrow in his voice, he said, "I'm sorry about Jessie and what her mother went through under my father's hand! I wish I knew sooner and would have helped but had no idea what I could have done. A sister would have been welcomed if I knew the truth."

Rose has not shared any of her Viking stories with Philippe. So, he was out of the loop with her feeling toward them. She saw the guilt he was carrying that was not his to bear. "Thank you, Philippe; I'm not sure what any of us could have done to change Jessie's situation. I do still miss her terribly. Please don't carry someone else's sins on yourself. You are too good a man for that. It's not the reason for me wanting to leave, but some of it, yes. I feel I need to go back - I belong there." For the first time, Rose opened up to him and explained as best she could, and he tried to understand.

"Does Antoine know you are leaving?"

"No, not yet. I promise to tell him soon, though I don't know how to break the news to him. I have no idea when the ship will return either, so it's a waiting game until then. However, there is more." Rose took a deep breath and explained why it was so crucial that Ollie would be leaving as well. He had to face his demons, much the same as Philippe was facing his right now.

"Wow! So Ollie is in line to be chief? It's almost the same as my status. So, he's kind of royalty as well – who knew? I guess he has no idea what's waiting for him on that side, and you haven't told him about his brother or mother's fate?"

"No, I beg you, please keep it between us for now. I should not be the person to tell him."

"You love him! I am happy for you, Rose." It was not a question but a statement. He could hear how she spoke about him. Rose did not want to think about her feelings for him right now. It would make it harder to let him go when he became chief.

Philippe wondered aloud, "Have you asked him why he left in the first place?".

Rose felt guilty for not thinking of it first. Why did she not think to ask why he left to understand Ollie's situation more. "No! It hasn't occurred to me to ask – until now. So much has happened, and it was a blow to find out who he really was. I tried to talk him into going because he refused to leave. I should have asked why he was feeling so negative about going back home! Oh, and now... you need him more than anything – I'm so sorry, Philippe! What will you do?"

"I'll be fine. He has to go; I know that. We will cope, I guess."

"Just don't rush into any marriages too soon; the matters of the heart are still vital even if you are king. Everything will work out for all of us." She was optimistic.

The next day Rose forced herself to tell Antoine. She organized a picnic for just the two of them and explained everything to him; she described her feeling towards Ollie and her love for the Vikings, which he already knew – Rose wanted him to understand her choices.

"It will be heart-rending to see you go, and maybe send an invitation soon if you can. You know I love adventures. Just think of what fun it would be."

"I'll be sure to make it on a festival; you have to experience that to believe it."

"Then it's a date. I'll be waiting for an invite. I've been meaning to tell you that while you were gone, I made a turn by Jessie's grave and found an old Indian woman there. I think it was her mother – we kind of spoke. I felt sorry for her, so I invited her to the kitchen for drinks and food. She seemed nice. I had nothing to say, so I left her there in the kitchen. She said she would leave as soon as she finished."

"Oh? I never knew she was here. I could have guessed she would visit Jessie's grave. She came to me first, and I told her where I buried Jessie. Her name is *Paytah*; it means fire." Rose smiled. "She blessed me with an Indian name as well; '*Ojinjintka*' Wildrose."

160

"The name suits you. The weird part in all this is – I think she might have poisoned my father! I can't be sure, but you know when you have that feeling…? I asked myself, what would I do to the person who killed my child and take revenge for what has been festering for so long?"

"Oh! Thinking about it now, when I asked her where she was, she said she had to settle something with an old friend that was left behind many moons ago. I really thought it was a friend. I don't know what to say to you, Antoine?"

"What can you say? My father's fate was sealed! He had that one coming to him, and his last actions just made it final."

"You have not told anyone?"

"No, that woman has been through enough, and she still mourns for her daughter. How can I? I told no one, not even Philippe – so please!"

"The secret is safe with me; if you are fine with it, then I'm fine with it."

When Orinn informed Philippe that he would be leaving, Philippe acted as if he was hearing it for the first time. He did not want to tell him that Rosaline explained everything to him already. If he had, Ollie would want to know what she said, and he did not want to lie to him. Philippe made it clear to Ollie that he was OK with him leaving so his conscience would be clean.

Orinn thought he was letting him down by leaving him so soon after all that's happened, especially considering the upcoming war. Ollie worked extra hard to get things done and passed out of exhaustion every night. He hardly saw Rose, only occasionally at breakfast or dinner.

10

*I*t was a hot and humid day, the coronation day; the castle was in turmoil with arrangements for the social gathering. The kitchen has been busy since early hours, and the church was preparing for the crowning ceremony. Antoine was helping the advisers with the documents that Philippe had to sign after he was crowned. Philippe made it clear to everyone that his brother was his right-hand man, his top adviser; thus, nothing gets approved without his consent or stamp of approval. Antoine was besieged with such a responsibility and was happy to please his brother, the king. Even though the church was packed, and the air was stuffy inside with the heat of the day, the coronation went well.

There was a roar of applause, and everyone left to attend the assembly to celebrate the joyous occasion. Philippe went with Antoine to sign the papers and joined the crowd afterward. At the main table, Philippe had his three most trusted friends – family. It was not much, but he was happy with them being there to support him. Léo was not allowed at the table. However, Philippe never really knew him, but knowing that he loved his brother, he would try to come to trust him too – if he could prove his loyalty.

Now that Philippe was king, he had to watch out for spies and anyone that wanted to harm him. He had to have two permanent guards on his tail at all times. Philippe made a private vow to himself and his brother that he would seek to earn his people's trust and loyalty. Antoine made another oath to always be by his side and help him become a great king.

Orinn and Rose sat next to each other. They made small talk explaining what their daily chores had been when arriving back. Rose could see it was bothering him to leave his new king, and so soon when he needed him the most. Ollie's duties still awaited him, and he had big choices to make for his own future.

A young servant girl was attempting to signal Rose but failed to do so. People were walking up to the table to congratulate the new king and bless him. Thus, she took the chance to see if that might help to get the lady's attention. Rose saw the girl smile and noticed she was making weird eye signals to her and was confused. The girl bowed to her new king, then said, 'God bless the king' and made one more eye contact with Rose. This helped the servant girl because Rose was now fixated on her.

Rose wondered what she was up to and followed her with her eyes. The girl stopped at the entrance door and turned to see if she still had Rose's attention. It worked – she signaled

Rose to meet her around the corner – curious as she was, Rose excused herself.

The servant was so relieved to get the lady's attention eventually; she never noticed that Orinn witnessed the exchange. He followed Rose in case there was trouble. He would have to tackle her afterward for being so gullible with strangers. The two women spoke, after which Rose followed her. They got on two horses and rode off. *What the hell is this woman up to? She's so stupid to just leave without any warning to her safety.* He was so angry he considered stopping her at first. However, he was curious himself about what all this sneaking around was.

He took the first horse he laid eyes on and followed the two. They stopped after a while, and the servant pointed at something and left Rose on her own. After riding further a few paces, Rose dismounted and walked further. He saw smoke coming through the trees where she entered and sneaked closer to investigate. Ollie saw Rose hug two men, upon which she started to cry. It was clear that these men camped here, and he could not understand the secrecy behind it all. Deciding to confront them, he left his cover, and when he came closer, having a better view, he immediately noticed their different clothing, instantly realizing who they were.

They all stared in shock at one another – Rose had no time to explain to Olaf and Var of the chieftain's lost son she found yet – and how dare he follow her! However, the damage was done. No introduction was needed even after all these years absent; they instantly knew who he was; Rose stood aside and let them be – immediately forgiving Orinn for his arrogance in following her.

"Olaf – Uncle Var?" *Rose said they were coming back, and they have.* There was a lot of back smacking, boasting and laughter. Olaf took out his mead, and they all drank around the fire. They asked many questions, and Orinn had to answer them all. When it was Orinn's turn to ask, there was silence, Rose knew they had to tell him, and it was time for her to leave.

"I'm going back to the celebrations so the three of you can catch up properly. I will return early tomorrow with breakfast. There will be plenty of leftovers after this evening. I'm thrilled to see you both again!" She bid them goodnight and left them to discuss what Orinn needed to hear.

When she returned to the castle, she told Antoine and Philippe about the new arrivals and that Ollie was with them. Her heart went out to Ollie with the sad news they were sharing about his family.

Philippe told her to send them an invitation from the king to attend a dinner that following evening. If Rose had high esteem for these people, then they should be good people. He would love to meet them and thank them in person for taking care of her when she needed it the most. Rose said she would pass on the message.

Before Rose retired that evening, with the celebration still going on, she went to the kitchen planning to pack a basket for her new visitors outside. There were only two servants left for the night to tidy up. Too tired and her mind on other things than food, she asked them politely to fill a basket with as many leftovers as possible and leave it on the counter; she'll pick it up early the next morning.

After a restless night, Rose was up early; she went to the kitchen, found two baskets full of food, and went on her way to meet her friends. When arriving, they had tea brewing and tucked in the food. She was pleased, and so were they with the bounty. Rose did not know how to start a conversation, nor had any idea how it went last night. She noticed Orinn never left as well, which was understandable - he looked tired!

"So..." she said to them.

Olaf spoke up next, "So Rose, have you packed yet?"

"What?"

"You are coming with - so we were told?"

"Yes—no - I mean, yes, I am, and no, I haven't packed yet." She was thrilled, and it showed.

"Sorry about your friend," Var said. Rose looked at Orinn, knowing a lot was said.

"Thank you, Var. She will be missed. I have an invitation for the two of you from our new king. You are to join us for dinner tonight at the castle."

"Oh really?" Olaf replied. Both Rose and Orinn said, "He's a good man."

They were reluctant to accept the invitation; however, Rose convinced them. Everyone in the castle was intrigued and fascinated with the new visitors. Nervous at first, however, they all fell in conversation with them when they saw how everyone was getting along. They were offered a room at the castle until their departure – when Rose and Orinn would be leaving with them.

At the dinner table, Antoine was seated next to Var, and they started speaking. Antoine liked him; even though he had a hard outer shell, he was a gentle soul. Philippe spoke to Olaf and liked his open personality. Even though he looked like a real roughneck, he could see he was an honest man, and his whole exterior said he was a true warrior. He would have loved to have him in his army, definitely in charge of them all.

There were many stares and giggles during the meal, watching how the two strangers ate their dinner. Some even joined in as fooling around and making fun, eating their meat with their hands. The two strangers weren't bothered as they weren't used to eating decently with utensils. They stayed for two days, then the four of them were on the road, ready for the voyage back home.

Helga was surprised to see Rose return to the ship – and she brought a visitor! When they told her who he was, she slapped him so hard on the back he stumbled, and everyone laughed. She was thrilled with the news. They were all settled on the ship, which Rose just heard for the first time was called a '*knörr*.' Olaf explained that they would be traveling faster and arriving home quicker if they were on a warship.

Rose asked why and he explained, "A warship, my lady, is narrower, longer and shallower than a '*knörr*' that is powered by oars. It is entirely open on deck, nothing else but the men standing in their gear and weapons ready for battle. Ah... those were great times, lass. Your blood pumping and your hearts are all in it, beating to the rhythm of the ocean.

"Hey – you are off course!" Rose laughed.

"What do you mean, lassy? We are on the right route. We can never get lost, and if we do, it's because it's done on purpose." He roared with laughter.

She laughed and said, "No, with your story about the two ships and how they differ! I would love to hear more about your war stories sometime, but first, the ships, please."

"Oh, OK... OK... now, where was I? Ah yes, only men standing and waiting for battle. The warship is called a '*langskip*.' It's built for speed and maneuverability, where a '*knörr*,' a merchant ship, is built for heavy cargoes and passengers. A warship can sail all the way up to the beach."

Rose interrupted him, "But this ship has holes for oars as well then?"

"Yes, my clever girl. The oars are used for maneuvering in preparation for landing only. I must add that this '*knörr*' can easily sail onshore as well; it was built that way. Our primary concern is our cargo. It is all nicely packed beneath us on soft hay. Now would you like to hear war stories?" He was eager to share with her.

Rose laughed and gave a big yawn. "Soon, I promise, it all sounds so exciting and intriguing. I would first love to enjoy the evening tonight, then rest my weary head. Tomorrow war stories, I will bug you until you tell them."

"No need, lassy, just bring mead, and it's done!" They all laughed.

Rose stood alone for a while, looking up at the many stars. There was a Milky Way tonight. The sights of such wonders always brought her closer to her God. Rose would sometimes look up and just say, *'Thank you!'*

Orinn walked towards her, "It's the most beautiful sight ever." Looking up and then at her.

Rose looked embarrassed and said, "I can share something about me that you don't know!"

"Oh yes, and what may that be?"

"You may not tell anyone; it's my secret I'm sharing with you! My favorite time is at night – and don't you laugh! I'm not a poet. However, I wrote a few poems when I was truly feeling down and lost at Jessie's place in the beginning."

"Please share one. I'm agog to hear one or two or even three..."

She laughed while saying, "Let me think of one first." Rose remembered them all but was unsure if she should share any. They were personal. *'Then why tell him!'* She thought.

Rose pointed her finger at him, "OK – no laughing!" and as a warning, showed her fist. She would punch him hard. "I was taught by the best." She pointed at Olaf.

Ollie's hands were up in surrender. "Oh, I see, then I shall try my best not to. A quick note before you go on, I just want to say that I see now what you meant about them being your family and how you are yourself with them. You are so different now, and they all adore you as well. OK, now you may continue."

Rose smiled and looked up at the heavens. The moon was perfect tonight – full – an enormous white shining marble in the sky. She explained first and said that all her poems come with a short explanation. He accepted it and waited.

"Well, I love looking at the moon. I always seek it out – it relaxes me by just staring at it. So, my Poem goes;

Full moon so bright,
Can you see me in your sight?
Big and round or small,
Sometimes behind a cloudy mall,
I always call on thee
To comfort me.

"Wow! That was not so bad, Rose! I'm now interested in hearing another."

"OK!" she smiled shyly, "As I said, I'm a night person. I love everything about it; it's cool and beautiful with the stars and the moon, the way they light up the darkness from above.

Spirit of the night
Guide me through
My future bright
Bless me whole
Guide my soul
—Why do I love thee oh night
Darkness, hide me insight
Moon and stars accompany me
They make me want to fly – to feel free...

Orinn had no words. They were profound and personal.

"I have one more to share with you that I wrote at Jessie's home before you came through. Then I'm done."

Star so bright
Star insight
Shine upon my soul tonight
And make it bright,
Take my fears out of sight
Bring happiness to my life.
—My heart is broken
My spirit is lost
My eyes are open – I see

My lips are moving,
But nothing to thee
What should I do
Or say to thee
  —Free me!

They both stood there looking out into the vast darkness of the ocean in silence. Orinn had nothing to say. He wanted to hold and kiss her so badly. However, he knew Rose would not allow it – not in front of the others.

Rose remembered Philippe's words and asked Orinn, "If you don't mind sharing some of your secrets, may I ask why you left in the first place?"

Orinn thought about that, and it was not a secret. He had never told anyone about it.

"Well, my father was all authority when I was young. He pushed me plenty to become tough, rough, and always ready for battles for my destiny to become chief one day. My siblings had it easy – they were carefree, I was allowed to join in their games at times, but not much. I heard my mother say to him that I was still a child, and if he pushed too hard, I might break. My father never agreed with her and said I was too soft; he believed in pushing hard, which he did, to toughen me up while I was still young enough to change into a strong man.

"The day he announced that I would be going on my first raid with them, my mother argued with him and said it was too soon for me to witness such acts. I thought I could handle it and said it was fine – wishing to please my father and put my mother at ease. My mother explained to me the reason why my father was so hard on me. She said he lost his parents at a young age, and if ever something should happen to him, I'd be ready to take charge. I was proud of my father, and I wanted him to be proud of me, to show him that I could stand as Chief one day.

"The raid was bountiful and with much violence that a child should not witness. I guess I was more my mother's child than my father's. We had the same traits of kindness. Although, what I saw as wrong, my father saw right. A Viking was a Viking, and they would never change. No one noticed I left early to return to the ship while they were still raiding.

"Upon arriving back home, they unloaded all the treasures they stole to share it amongst the two tribes. The other tribe grabbed some villagers for slaves, and between them, I found a young girl. I was so angry and disgusted that anyone would think of stealing a child away from its home just to be a slave to please them. I took her and confronted my father with all I had in me – I stood up to him. He was not happy and shouted back, but I stood my ground.

"The girl was terrified and stood behind me while I confronted him. She never uttered a sound or even cried? I thought maybe she was still in shock, or there might be something mentally wrong with her. My father said it was none of our business and to leave it at that – but I did not! I took the

174

child to my aunt's house and told her to please keep her until I decided what to do.

"They drank on for days and totally forgot about the girl. When I heard about the next raiding trip, I decided to return the girl home or try to anyway. I had no idea where she lived. All I knew was where they raided, so taking her back there, she might find her own way, or if someone knew her, they would take her home. My aunt drugged her to sleep, to relax on our voyage. I was hoping she would not make a sound, and she did not. I was told to give her more medication after her meals. But once on the road, it was not necessary."

At this point, Rose was transfixed and just stared at him, hanging on to every word.

While Orinn was explaining, he was leaning on the rails, staring ahead into the darkness over the vast ocean, lost in his own memory, — "When we were anchored, and the crew was all passed out, I took a dingy from the ship and rowed to shore. We walked for a very long time until we came to a town. The girl made a sound for the first time since being with her and started walking towards a house. I stood looking at how she was carried in. It made me feel good inside for doing a deed that I decided never to go back - being a Viking was not for me. My father would be upset, but I thought my mother would understand. I mentally apologized to my aunt because she thought I was returning; that's why she helped. She, too, felt sorry for the young child.

175

"Afterward, I went and lived by an old tribe that lived nearby the same seashores all their lives. A gentle tribe; never looked for trouble with anyone. I stayed there for a few years before I returned to France. I walked on for days, restless, looking for work. I stumbled upon an elderly man fixing his wagon wheel, then by some miracle, he invited me to his home and offered me a job, and that's where I have been until I lost everything that was dear to my heart. I married his daughter; she was pregnant before the sickness came and lost them both. Soon afterward, I joined the army." There was silence before he stood straight and faced her. "That's it - my whole life up to now, so to say!"

Rose was thinking of another story that Jessie told her.

"It was me!"

He was still so engrossed in his story that he did not understand her. "Excuse me?"

"The girl was me! I was three years old. I don't remember that that ever happened to me and still can't remember even after hearing it for the second time."

Ollie said, "I know or thought it could be you when we went to your house for the first time together, but I wasn't sure."

"Jessie said no one knows how I got back, and that's why my mother colored my hair lest they were searching for me. It was you... you risked everything and gave up your destiny to save a young girl. Thank you! I don't think I would have been happy as a slave. Who knows what would have happened to me with the other tribe?" Rose was thinking of her attacker. "Now it's my turn to help you where I can."

She thought of the tribe he went to stay at first and was curious.

"The water tribe you went to live by for a few years – is that where you got your last name? I know Vikings don't have last names, so I was just wondering if that's where you got yours?"

He laughed, "Yes. They have always lived there and never moved. Some people mixed with the regular town folks, and a few even moved into the town itself. When they realized people were using a last name, they created one for themselves – Waters – because of the location and being so close to the water all the time."

"Oh... That's very interesting! So, they are starting to live in ordinary towns now?" Rose was astonished.

"Yes, two or three families have started. They always lived not far from the town, mingled with the people, and traded when the town started to expand. They are different from most Vikings. It's a small tribe that never raided in their lives; therefore, the town folks trusted them, not like the others you hear about. As I said, they are different from most Vikings and their ways. To be honest, I cannot see this happening with the other tribes, though."

"Yeah..." She could not see it either.

They were a few hours away from the island, and everyone on board was excited to be nearly home. Their trading voyage was long and productive, and now they missed their families. Except for Orinn, his nerves were on end. He had no idea how his reunion would be once he arrived.

Rose noticed and tried to reassure him and decided a distraction might help a little to ease his tension. So, she fetched a bottle of mead and gave it to Olaf, then asked, "Would you please tell us more stories of the war and how your ships worked in battle?"

He was eager to comply. "Our warships were the best - are the best! We had about twenty-four men at the oars on each ship. Our goal was to conquer the enemy ship without harming the ship itself, only the crew. Their loss was our gain. We would empty their ship of all crew and then claim it as bounty with all that was on board. By achieving this, we would tie the two ships together and use a sturdy walking plank to form an island between the two, then the battle would begin, or it had already begun; spears and swords everywhere. Our ships could maneuver in the shallowest places that no one would expect or think it was possible to land, which gave us an upper hand in secrecy and always had the advantage. Ah... those were the days. What I wouldn't give for just one more battle to cool my blood," he laughed out loud.

They were nearing the island by now, and everyone was silently looking ahead.

They docked, and some of the crews' family was there to greet them. Rose saw that Popi and her family were not there, probably waiting for Var to come home. Everyone was surprised to see Rose return and greeted her with pure joy. When they walked past the central part of the village to the main house, everyone noticed the stranger and wondered who he was. Anyone who knew Thord could see that this man looked familiar. Var, Olaf and Rose walked in with Orinn waiting to see the chief. He was in a meeting with one of the villagers. Olaf went in first before they all entered.

"Chief." Olaf wasn't sure how he was going to give the news to his chief yet. He would have to say it as it is and take the heat if there was any.

"Olaf, how were your travels, my good man?" While they were gone, the chief had actually been considering electing Olaf to be the next chief. Since he was born, he'd been part of his family, and his parents were his mentors and meant a lot to him. Kiti was not going to marry anytime soon, and she seemed very unhappy these days. He couldn't think of any way to cheer her up and felt at a loss. Perhaps if Olaf became chief, Thorarin could think of going on a trading tour and taking Kiti along. He knew that it would please her to get off this island and see new things.

Olaf answered, "It was gratifying, chief. We picked up many new materials for the women and plenty more different spices. The trade went well, and may I say, on our way home, we added two more passengers."

"What do you mean? Has Rose been dropped off, and have you seen to her safe passage to the people she was intended to go to?"

"Yes, chief. Rose was our first and primary concern before our travels. She was so distraught that we promised to return before coming home again to see if she was OK. Although, once there, we ran into a new friend of hers. We were also invited to the castle for dinner and stayed there until we were ready to leave. I must say that Rose went through a lot in that short time, and with this new friend, we decided to bring them both back."

"Olaf, you have me confused? You brought Rose back, and on top of that, another stranger; a friend she made in that short time she has returned home?"

"Yes, chief. That sounds about right."

"Well, don't have me hanging here in suspense; who is this new person then?" He was getting irritated that he wouldn't come right out and say who this person was.

"Chief – they are both waiting outside with Var. I thought I'd come in first to tell you so the blow would not be that bad. It's your son, Orinn." Olaf waited for a response but got none.

The chief seemed to freeze with emotion. He shifted in his seat and said in a calm voice, "Let them in." He could not or did not know how to respond to this news; his son, who left one day without any word or reason, has returned. He felt angry, sad, and happy all at the same time, and that's how his emotions played out, in that order.

180

Olaf opened the door, and Var was the first to enter; Rose followed suit, and Orinn walked in last. They were all four standing and staring at the chief, waiting for him to say something; Chief Thorarin was at a loss for words. Rose decided to greet him; the chief was honestly happy to see her again and welcomed her back. He greeted Var as well and stared at his son again; his emotions were building up. Rose and Var took a step back for father and son to speak.

"Hello, father," was all Orinn said.

The chief seeing his son for the first time in so many years; always wondered where he was or if he was still alive. It was torture, and now he was standing in front of him, no longer a young boy, but a man, alive and healthy, and all he had to say was '*Hello, father!*' His anger boiled; you could see him going red.

"Hello, father? Where the hell were you all these years, and why the hell did you leave without saying a word to your mother or me? Do you know what you put us through, not knowing where you were or if you were still alive and well – especially your mother? The thought of you out there all alone! How could you do this to us?" His anger was a roar that bounced off the walls.

It shook Rose so severely that her whole body shivered, and just then, all the memories of that time of her first abduction came flooding back to her. The same incident as when she was a child and a young boy who stood up for her, she hid behind him, yet again. She was transfixed on the spot with the new memory standing behind Orinn. No one noticed.

Orinn was not surprised by his outburst. He expected as much and stood his ground. He felt sad for his mother's loss, but he could do nothing to change that now. If he could, he would have at least discussed this with her. He was young, scared, and not ready for the life he was brought up to follow.

"I'm sorry for what I've put you and mother through, and I'm truly sorry to hear about her demise. It was just a decision that came to me once I finished my course of action to save that young girl who was kidnapped."

"What are you talking about?"

"I still came to you that night when we returned after my first raid. I was unhappy with what I saw, then still coming back and seeing a three-year-old child taken as a slave. I came to you and told you that it was wrong and that she had to be taken back. Taking an adult was still OK to be a thrall, but a baby? It just made no sense to me and said this much to you. You answered that it was not your or our problem and that the other tribe will handle it. I was upset and made a plan to return her, but once there, I decided on a different future for me than the one you had planned. I was proud and still am to be a Viking, but to have no feelings for others was not me.

"After what I saw and knew what you expected of me – I knew you would not understand. Sorry father, I was young at the time, and I must admit, I was not thinking of my actions and how it would affect you and mother. That is my deepest

182

regret, and I can never get that moment with her again." Ollie looked heartbroken that his mother was gone. He always believed he would see her again.

Chief Thorarin's emotions were all over the place, losing his wife, then his son long before his time, and now his lost son returning home – he had tears in his eyes. He never knew Orinn felt that way and knew he was right about not understanding then. He would have been harder on him and pushed him more. His wife knew better; he should have listened to her when she said it was not time yet to introduce him to the Viking way. Thorarin blamed himself for not listening to his son more. The chief was thrilled to see him again and proud of the man that stood before him; no matter his choices, he was just happy that he has returned.

He stood up and walked to stand in front of his son; he grabbed and hugged his son for the first time and held him close before letting go again. Var and Olaf, as big grown men that they were, were close to tears themselves.

After all the suspense and drama playing before them between father and son, Var eventually noticed that Rose was not herself. When he walked towards her, that's when everyone else noticed as well. She stood frozen in one spot. Var, not knowing what to do, shook her out of her quiescent state.

"Rose, Rose... Are you alright?" Var looked worried.

Rose looked up at him and then at everyone else and said, "I remember – I remember everything now!"

"What do you remember, Rose?" Var thought she lost it again.

She looked at Orinn. "When I was taken for the first time!" Rose looked at the chief, "No wonder your voice shook me so badly when I met you for the first time and fainted! It was a memory I was holding back for so many years, and now with that outburst of yours – it returned!"

They all laughed at her for being so overconfident with the chief. Except for the chief himself, Thorarin had no idea what she was talking about. Neither did the other two, but just the way she spoke made them snort.

She looked at Orinn and smiled, "I remember!"

"I'm glad!" He returned the smile.

The chief was a little annoyed at this time and asked what returned.

"Father, this is going to shock you!" Orinn looked at the other two and said, "The two of you as well. Remember I said I took a girl back to her island after we abducted her. Well..." he looked at Rose, and they all looked at her as well, "It was Rose!"

All three said in unison, "No!"

Just then, Popi came storming into the room. She heard from others the ship has returned and waited patiently for her husband to walk through the door. Time went by, and she was wondering what was taking so long. She got worried and hoped it wasn't another attack on their vessels with many injured. She rode as fast as she could to the village, then heard that Rose was back as well and wondered what happened. Popi was over-excited to see her again and thought this day would never come. She rushed inside the main house, ready to lash out at everyone for not letting her know or call on her.

Rose ran straight into her arms when she entered; all ill words were gone from her lips. Popi hugged her child back and held her tight. She walked over to her husband, greeted him, and then looked at the strange man standing there. It took her three seconds to know who he was, and her legs gave way. Her hands grabbed her heart; she gave a deep moan and cried out loud, "Orinn, are my eyes deceiving me? Is this really you, my child – have you returned home at last?"

Orinn was overjoyed to see his favorite aunt again and went over to hug her. "Yes, it's really me, Aunt Popi." The whole room was joyous; everyone was talking at once. The chief ordered mead for them all, and Var enlightened Popi with some news.

"My sweet love, you remember many moons ago when you looked after a young pup for young Orinn?"

"Oh, my husband, you are going back many years now – but yes, I do and will never forget that time. Why do you ask?"

"Hold on to your seat, my love, because that little girl was our Rose you protected then."

"What – don't speak lies to me; I'm too old for such nonsense!"

"No lies, Aunt Popi, it's true!" Orinn and Rose explained; Popi was stunned to hear this and happy that it was Rose that she protected then and now. She had a feeling when Sigrid cut Rose's hair for the first time; however, she dismissed it. It was impossible that the same little girl then would have somehow returned and would not believe it.

Orinn spoke to his father about Thord and how sorry he could not meet him as a man today. He still remembered the little boy running around and being up to no good. They spoke a few minutes about Thord then he asked where Kiti was. His father explained that she has not been feeling herself, and he has no idea how to bring her out of this state.

Orinn left to personally meet his baby sister in private. He was excited to see her again and felt sad that it could not be under different circumstances, where he was greeting his brother too. He was gone for over an hour. During that time, the news spread that the eldest son has returned, and a celebration was planned. They organized a festival in rapid time. Everyone was there outside the main house. Fires were started, tables were decorated, and the festivity began. Sigrid and Cnut were ecstatic to see Rose again and never left her side that day. She was over the moon to be back *home*.

Kiti came down with Orinn; her eyes were still red and swollen from all the crying. Orinn's eyes were also red. She was holding on to him the whole time. Arms hooked in Orinn's, Kiti walked over to where Rose was standing.

"Hello Rose, I'm pleased to see you again and glad you have returned. You were strangely missed." She smiled kindly at Rose, and Rose thanked her. They had an awkward hug, then

Kiti was hooked in Orinn's arms again. Orinn and Rose were separated the whole evening, mingling with the crowd. Many questions were thrown at Orinn and Rose. '*Where have you been – what were you up to – is it true about Rose?*' Were the many questions that were asked of Orinn.

'*What happened to you – where did you stay – how was it there – and is it true about you being here as a baby?*' were the many questions that were thrown at her. News did travel fast on this small island, and they answered all to the many inquisitive minds until they were all appeased. It was a joyous occasion that lasted until the early hours of the morning. Rose was sleeping at Popi's place this time and was happy to be walking that path again with everyone who saw her off last time.

Orinn retired early, leaving with his father and sister. Rose let them be. They had many things to discuss and catching up to do in private as a family. She, of all, knew that feeling.

11

*R*ose woke up smiling, feeling refreshed; thankfully, she did not have much to drink. She was where she had been pining to be since leaving, where her heart was – back home! She had many stories still to share with Popi and Sigrid, but most of all, she could not wait to get back to work and feel needed again.

They all had their breakfast, talking and laughing happily. They were about to ask more questions about her time at the castle when they received an early visitor. Ollie walked in; he greeted Var and hugged Popi. Sigrid was still a young pup when he saw her last and could not believe how she grew.

"And who may this young man be?" Looking at Cnut.

Popi laughed, "That's our youngest. You weren't here when he was born. I was pregnant when you left those years."

"I did not know!"

"We told no one until we were certain ourselves."

Orinn spoke to Cnut, "Well, my young man, I'm pleased to meet a new cousin of mine. I hope to see more of you, and we can spend some time together."

Cnut just smiled politely and nodded. Losing Thord was difficult, and now this stranger was in his place - something to get used to.

Var greeted him and was off to the fields once again, with Cnut following behind him.

Orinn spoke to Sigrid and Rose when Popi asked, "Have you eaten my boy? There are plenty leftovers."

"No, thank you, my aunt. I've come seeking Rose and would like a word in private if that is fine? They all stared at Rose, and she stood up.

The two women cleared the table to wash up while Orinn and Rose took a walk.

Once alone, walking not far from the house in the woods - he confided in Rose. "I'm sorry we had no time to be together last night!"

Rose smiled, "We've had many before. I understand how it should be for the three of you after so many years. You don't need to explain to me."

"I do, Rose! My father and I had many words to say to each other in private. It was a long, exhausting discussion. One you know about; me to be chief! He wants to know how I feel about that and how my views are on being back."

"And - what did you say?"

"I was honest with him and said I was not sure. I'm back for not even a day, and this was thrown on me."

Rose could see he was confused with this new responsibility in his life, and returning after so long was still something to get used to. Seeing his family again and being welcomed with open arms, his emotions were all over the place.

"I told you, you had to come back, that they needed you. To have in mind too that you would be chief. So, in truth, you knew this was coming – so what's really the issue? No one can force you to stay if you don't want to, and to accept that offer is a huge responsibility and respect to your father. It is your destiny! Things have changed since last you've been here."

"I know; I can see that it has. I'm just not sure I'm ready to be chief and to take on that task so soon?"

"You can, and what do you mean so soon?"

"He wants to step down as soon as possible and announce me chief. He wants to do it before the next festival. I knew my father would expect this of me after hearing of Thord's passing, but not so soon! I was thinking that he would let me slowly work my way into it and getting to know things first."

"So, you decided already that you would be chief. I don't understand why you are afraid – it will come to you naturally, you will see, everything will be fine!"

He grabbed her with an overpowering urge and kissed her with a hunger he had never felt before. He needed to feel her close and taste her again. She responded with the same eagerness. Rose, of all people, knew this would not last and could not go on for long. She honestly loved him and was so proud of him for coming back and facing his fate. Except, now that they were back, she was still an outsider and could not have any relations with a Viking. Rose broke the kiss and pushed him away with tears in her eyes.

"Orinn, this can't go on! This, which we are feeling and doing, must stop for you to become the chief your father can be proud of."

"What are you talking about, Rose? You will always be by my side and be mine – no one will stop me!"

"No! Don't say things like that. Your father needs you, and I need you to make him proud. He's been through so much in a short time, and what I heard, the loss of your mother broke the man you knew those years – he still feels her loss. And not to mention the pain he must still be feeling for losing a child so soon too, I can see the pain in his eyes for not having Thord around anymore. He needs this to happen, and so do you. I'm an outsider that can't be involved with you, you of all being chief. I do love you so much, and it hurts like hell to say this to you, but until you become chief, we can't see each other again, and hopefully, our feelings will have changed by then!"

"But Rose, that's not why I came to talk to you, and I never want to hear you utter those words again about you being an outsider. I see how these people love and accept you as their own; why can't you see that? You have always been part of my plans in my life, and I'm so glad to hear you love me. I love you more than I care to say."

"Please don't, Ollie! You cannot dishonor your father. I will not be the cause to break up a father and son so soon after their reunion." Rose ran away, leaving him stunned. Those words meant more to her than any uttered in a long time. To feel that she belonged as one of them was all she ever wanted; however, she knew it was not true. Just knowing that he loved her back made it more complex; her heart was breaking. She needed to get away before making any plans to run away with him – just to be together.

Rose knew how it should be – she learned that with Thord. Thord had done everything to please his father. Now she understood why; his brother Orinn dishonored their father, hurt him so much. Thord was witness to that pain and vowed never to hurt him. Thord knew what this meant for him to become chief and make his father proud. Now it was Orinn's time to heal that pain. To make amends and resume Thord's role where he left off.

Rose ran all the way home and straight into Popi's arms, crying. All Popi could do was console her, not knowing what happened between Orinn and herself. When her sobbing subsided, Rose would not speak of it and said she was fine. She did not want Popi or the others to know how she felt over Orinn. It was a battle of the heart she would have to surmount on her own. That night after dinner, as always, Var made a fire, and this time, it was Rose's turn to tell a story. She spoke of her dear friend Jessie and the fate that had awaited her.

No one left until she was done with the story, and they all commented on the subject. They offered condolences and were still speechless with the twist in it. Var was satisfied with the fate of the king and said justice was served. Popi loved the name the Indian woman blessed her with; *'Ojinjintka'* (Wildrose). She felt sorry for Rose and everything she experienced there. She was proud of her survival skills and even more swollen with pride that she remembered everything she was taught. Therefore, each night after dinner, Rose was questioned about her time there until she ran out of stories.

*I*t had been a week since she last spoke to Orinn and had not seen him since either. Rose was confused with her feelings. She told him to stay away until after the coronation, so why was she upset about it? What did she expect from him – to come running to her and carrying her out into the sunset – please! He was a Viking now and should be as Thord was, proud and honored to be chief. Rose knew this was going to happen, and still, it did not make it easier. For the first time, her feelings went against the Viking rules, and she wished they had stayed at Jessie's place or the castle – anywhere so they could be together.

When Rose ran away and left Orinn alone in the woods, he badly wanted to run after her and reassure Rose that his feelings for her would never change. No matter what happened or who he became, he would always love her. Rose had strong feelings and words to say about his father. She truly respected the chief and cared for his happiness, to give up love so that he could become chief and make his father proud. He loved her even more for her sacrifice to please others. He let her go and slowly walked back to the main house. He had a lot to think about on his walk and a great deal more to say to his father. He would have to call on Popi and Var at a later date to speak to them too. His mind was made up; if his father disapproved, then it was his loss.

Orinn explained to his father how he felt about Rose and everything she went through back at the castle. He told him how she spoke of them and how she respected him and how willing she was to give up their love to please him more than anyone else.

The chief could not believe what he was hearing. He was not surprised they fell in love; he actually liked Rose a lot. He never knew Rose felt so strongly for his kind. He had always thought she just loved Popi and her family because of her loss, never further than that. The chief had been blind to the truth, first, his son's feelings when he was young and now this - when will he ever learn? Thorarin felt in his heart that his wife would have approved of Rose, and so he gave his blessing for their betrothal. He asked one thing of his son before he announced the news.

"I ask that you keep this to yourself until after the coronation, and then you can do as you please. Rose is going nowhere; they say absence makes the heart grow fonder. I will call on Var and Popi in the days close to your coronation so you can speak to them, but they too must keep this secret. This is all I ask of you."

"I will respect your wishes until then, father." Ollie was satisfied and would keep his word.

Two days before the coronation, Var and Popi were called in secretly to see the chief in a private meeting. They entered the Chief's sitting room - at a loss as to why they were summoned. They all greeted, and Orinn asked them to sit.

"Uncle Var and Aunt Popi, my father has not called you, but I have; I need to ask you a serious question!" They both sat up straighter, not sure where this was going.

"You are the closest thing as parents Rose has; she loves you very much, and I know the feeling is mutual. As such, you speak for her; that's why I have called on you. I want your blessing on asking Rose for her hand in marriage and hope you approve of me. I promise to always be there for her and make her happy as best as I can. To be the husband she deserves." He waited for their answer.

They both looked at the chief, and he nodded in approval. Var slapped his knee and laughed. Popi got up, hugged Orinn, and cried, "I think I speak for both of us when I say we would be honored that you will care for our Rose as we do and love her as she deserves to be loved. I could not think of a better man for her." Var and Orinn shook hands, and then the chiefs. Orinn informed them that it should stay between them until after his coronation, and they accepted.

Var had to ask, "So how does this work? What kind of wedding will this be?" He would not dare go further than those words, although, knew this had to be asked.

The chief spoke and surprised them all, "This will be treated as it is, a Viking wedding and respected as such. It's no use avoiding the fact that she is one of us, not by blood, but definitely by heart."

Var was happy with the answer, and Popi was over the moon. There was much to be done, but for now, that had to wait. A dowry was made to finalize the deal until they were both satisfied. Popi could not share this great news with Rose, which she knew would make her very happy. She could see the girl was down and very depressed. All Popi could say and dare to say to her was, *'Never doubt that you are not one of us. We love you as our child and will always see to your happiness.'*

*O*n the day of the coronation, everyone was busy preparing for the main event. The ceremony would be inside the main hall where it should be held and then celebrated outside with games, dares and competitions. A chief only becomes a chief after the old one dies or is unfit, and another is nominated as head chief. This was a little new to what they were used to.

Thorarin had it different. It had been a long process that he went through after his father died before he became chief. The hour was upon them, and Chief Thorarin was seated on his main stool. Everyone that was everyone was there. Orinn, his son, walked forward and stood in front of his father.

Thorarin stood up and spoke up for all to hear, "I as chief have been chief after my father and his before him. It has been in our family for generations; we always stood up to that honor to lead our people and care for them. Not one generation has failed to appease our people, and I ask you my son, Orinn. Will you take this honor and stand before me and all these witnesses and swear that you will honor my blood by following in our good name to lead our people so I can step down and be proud?"

"I accept the honor and privilege to rule after you, my chief. I will lead our people as you have and your fathers have done to the best of my knowledge."

Chief Thorarin offered his son a white feather for purity and honesty, and he accepted it. They shook hands and hugged; they turned and exchanged places, where the father faced his son - the new chief. Now Orinn stood where his father stood and felt the pride for the first time. His father motioned him to sit, and he stepped back. The old chief could not be more complacent where he was standing and feeling incredibly proud of his son.

The day went swimmingly well, and the games began. The celebrations would last for three days, then two weeks' hard work on the island for everyone for the next festival. Everyone congratulated the new chief. They all said that this day would always be remembered and that it would be written in the books. Their new chief was named after their chief god, Odin, and they felt they were blessed from this day on. They knew the gods were celebrating too with this event.

For the first time since last they spoke in the woods, Orinn and Rose saw each other in the hall before the event started. They both greeted each other with smiles, and her heart almost stopped.

Rose witnessed the event with Popi and her family. In the end, the roar of applause was thunderous. She left the hall early for some fresh air and could not face him now or speak to him. She would wait until everyone had their moment and then try. Rose wanted this for him and the villagers; they all needed hope, which Rose received when she first came here. This was his destiny, and now she felt at a loss as to hers.

What will she do with her future ahead? She could not marry a Viking or see herself happy with a thrall, and to see him getting married one day to someone else would break her. Should she stay? The feeling of leaving left an ache in her heart; this was her home now, although, if she wished, she could always leave and go back to the castle.

Rose would always be welcomed there, and Antoine would be happy to see her. Rose was strained on what would make her happy. Not so long ago, she had wanted a man that was not available to her, and the thought of losing another love broke her. Rose decided she needed a distraction and went home to make concoctions for the surely coming injuries. She would congratulate Orinn later when she had time.

The distraction did help a little, and later in the day, Sigrid came to help Rose. She spoke of what happened so far, the games that were won, and everyone saying Chief Orinn this and Chief Orinn that – and was laughing with joy. She asked Rose why she wasn't enjoying the day with the others.

Rose tried to laugh it away, "I thought it was best to make ointments for the injuries, and you know how that goes during these events; it's a full day's job. I am very happy for Orinn, the old chief and the villagers. I will join in the games myself tomorrow and have some fun – I promise!" Rose still had her bow and arrow that Olaf made for her and would try it out tomorrow for the first time again. She will have a few drinks and really try to be happy and enjoy the day, except she needed this time for herself.

Orinn was so busy on the first day that he had no time for himself or to go in search of Rose. He heard she was busy with ointments and such and thought he would have time later. It was very late in the evening when he asked Popi where Rose was, and she said that Rose retired early but will be joining in the fun tomorrow. Orinn was a little disappointed and needed to speak to her, but decided it could wait until the morrow. He went on drinking with Olaf and the rest of the villagers who were still celebrating.

Early the following day, Rose took her bow and tested it out in the garden. She was a little out of practice, yet knew she would get the hang of it soon. She took out the dress Popi made for her at her last festival. She felt good about this day. After a few practice rounds, Rose and Sigrid went out to start the day and had a hearty breakfast first. Popi and the rest followed soon afterward. Rose had a few drinks and was getting into the day's events with much laughter. Olaf and Helga were cheering her on the whole time.

Orinn was not used to these celebrations and slept late. When he eventually woke and joined the festivities again, he was stunned to see Rose in the competitions and doing well with the bow. The sight of her stopped him in his tracks. She looked more stunning than he cared to remember, with her hair all loose and in a joyous mood – and the way she was dressed made his heart skip a beat. He knew he could never love another the way he loved her at that very moment. He sat down with Popi and cheered Rose on as well. He will wait until after the games to speak to her. No one and nothing could stop him now.

Rose saw Orinn and heard him applaud her. She felt so relaxed that she actually waved at him. After the games, she went with Cnut and Sigrid for more drinks and to mingle. She was standing and speaking to Astrid, Popi's eldest daughter, and oohing over her new baby in her arms when Rose heard her name being called out. She turned and saw Orinn walk towards her, and smiled, and greeted him in his status.

"Good day, Chief Orinn – congratulations!"

He could not wait and was straight to the point. These last days waiting up to now was torture not seeing her – as he promised his father, he would not till he becomes chief.

"Rose, I need to ask you something. Please hear me out before you answer." He was nervous and wanted this done. He could not spend another day without her by his side; he was also scared that he might frighten her away again. Thus, he spoke from his heart.

Rose wondered what he was talking about. "You look so serious – is everything alright?"

"Everything is fine." Orinn took her hands and spoke, "Rose, remember when we laid on your floor in Jessie's house? I could not sleep that night with you in my arms and kept staring at you. The feeling of not having you in my life, close to me all the time – scared me. I knew then that we belonged together, and I would do anything to make that happen, and I know you feel the same. I thought carefully about what to say so you could see how I feel about you. I already know my heart belongs to you, and I will lose my mind if we spend another day apart. I want to spend the rest of what I have with the woman I love."

Rose became nervous, looked around, and saw that everyone was staring. "Orinn, please stop!"

"No, Rose, we only have one life on this earth, and my life belongs with you! I'm not used to these celebrations and drinking through the night, and I know I consumed too much last night, but my mind is clear about how I feel about you. I want to live with you, and I want to love you until our lives end and into the next. Rosaline Dumont, will you marry me – take me as your husband?"

Orinn waited for an answer, and Rose just stared in shock and awkwardness. She looked anxiously at the old chief, and he was smiling – does this mean he accepts this proposal? She looked at Popi, and she was nodding all the time – if it were not so serious, Rose would have laughed out loud. She looked around, and not just Orinn, but everyone was waiting for her to answer. '*Was it OK to say yes – is this really happening to me?*'

"You know how I feel about you, but I don't understand what's happening – is this allowed?"

"I am the new chief with new rules; it's my decision to take you as my wife if you agree? Popi and Var stand as your family; they have blessed this arrangement – it's up to you now?"

Would she dare...? "Yes!" Orinn grabbed Rose and kissed her in front of all; the applause was loud and jubilant. She pushed him away and was scarlet with embarrassment.

"You can't do this! You can't declare your love for me without everyone thinking you know what, and you are dishonoring my family." She remembered the story Popi told and what everyone must be thinking. It was said terrible things would happen to the man. Rose wanted to laugh at the silly notion herself.

Orinn roared with laughter and kissed her again, and again she pushed him away laughing. Rose stared into his eyes and saw the love in them. This time, she kissed him. There was a new cause for celebration and congratulations. Rose could not believe this was happening; it all felt like a dream – a dream she never wanted to wake from. The old Chief Thorarin walked up to Rose, and many heard what he had to say.

"Congratulations, Rose; I know you will make my son happy. You are not a Viking by blood, but you definitely proved that you are a Viking by heart, and that is as strong and good enough for me. Welcome to our family."

He meant family as everyone else was on the island, not just his, and she knew that. Rose was so touched by his words, and as only she could show her thanks, she jumped up and hugged him, and the people around laughed and cheered once again.

Rose had to talk to Orinn about something important. She was honored to be part of these peoples' lives and be one of them, although something was bothering her. She always respected their ways, traditions, and religion, but she would never change who she was or what she believed in. Rose had one God, and it says in the Bible that He's a jealous God. She would not want to be on His wrong side by choosing or praising other gods or false gods, not even in the name of love, not that theirs were false, and she would never say that to them. She never judged a person in her life. Therefore, she explained to him and asked if it was required from her now that she was seen as a Viking.

"Rose, you forget that I never actually grew up here, though I grew up believing in them. Once out there, you learn other facts and come to believe in the truth. I too believe in one God, and no, no one expects you to give up what you believe in."

Rose was relieved and smiled at her handsome husband-to-be. Popi and her family came over to congratulate them, and she was straight in Popi's arms, hugging her dear old friend.

12

Close to two weeks had passed since Orinn became chief and proposed to Rose. Rose still stayed with Popi's family, and they were all preparing for the upcoming wedding. Rose was nervous and excited as the day grew nearer. Orinn came over to see her every day, or when she was helping in the village; he would steal her away for a few seconds. Astrid, Sigrid and Popi were making her wedding dress, and Rose was not allowed to help! Not that it was a tradition for other women to make it. They knew Rose could not sew and gave her other tasks.

She was happy to comply; being occupied kept her nerves at bay. Sometimes she would relax and chitchat with them while they were sewing. She loved what they had done so far; Popi was happy with the new materials, which Var brought back on their last trade mission. They had silk, satin, and lots of lace to work with. Vikings love colorful clothing; the more you stand out, the better. Popi preferred a white dress with lots of lace; white for purity and innocence was perfect for her Rose.

They made an outfit for Orinn as well and used more of a light cotton material for his. It was more an off-white, close to a light beige color – a loose pants with an open sleeve shirt tied at the chest – loose strings. Rose's dress was made of silk and was long and slick; with long sleeves, the edges were made of lace to cover half of her hands. She had a V-neck, which was covered in lace to cover the neck. They made a unique design at the back of the dress with extra-long lace, dragging on the floor, which could be removed after the wedding.

It was now all done, and they all waited for the day to arrive. The wedding would take place a week during the festival. Everything was done in the nick of time for the coming celebration that would be held first.

It was the first ritual that Orinn had participated in and had the honor to take his late younger brother's place at the Altar. Olaf took over that role, and now it was Orinn's place to bring a young sheep to be offered to their chosen gods. The old chief still had the leading authority in the Altar. When it was time, it would be passed on to Orinn; he still had much to learn as he had not been present for many years and forgotten most of the blessings and prayers performed on the Altar or how it should be done. Vikings believed in things being done correctly, especially if it's to their gods to appease them or bad omens would befall the island's people.

After the slaughter, Orinn felt blessed to be home with his family again, and the sacrifice went well. Everyone was happy and ready for the new season celebration to begin. Popi and Sigrid had their hands full trying to keep the two lovebirds separated most of the time and always be present – Sigrid failing hopelessly in that duty. They could not be left alone until their wedding day arrived and took that serious, though Ollie was a hand full, which Popi always had more words to throw his way, but all in all, it was all done in good humor, love, and appreciation that they had a new chief and soon a wedding to celebrate as well. There was much laughter and more than only a mere celebration to toast.

A week after the season celebration, the wedding day was set on a Friday – 'Frigg's day' – a tribute to Frigg, the goddess of marriage. A Viking wedding was beautiful, and no matter how it was performed, if it was done in love and truth and in front of her God, then it was sacred enough. Rose looked stunning that morning, all dressed up, and Popi was in tears. Rose had a permanent smile on her face that would not disappear.

When Cnut came and announced everything was ready and Orinn was waiting, they all walked with her to her wedding. It was held outside, the same as when Olaf was married. Rose walked up slowly towards Orinn; he complimented her on her looks – she was glowing. They were both ready for this day and for this to happen. No cold feet or second thoughts, both were going into this with open hearts. Everyone attended would be witness to their joint union. The old chief stood in front of them to pass on the necessary items for their ceremony. Var and Popi were not far to lend a hand if needed. Orinn gave Rose his ancestral sword; she would pass it down to their firstborn son. Var gave Rose a sword, which he made for her to pass on to Orinn.

On it was his family crest as she was now part of the family; she offered this to him. Next, rings were given; a stand was built to place the swords' sharp end in, and the rings were tied with a neat bow on top. It emphasized the sacredness of the union. They took their rings, and each had a turn to place the rings on their fingers while reciting their vows. They kissed, and the great feast began.

From this day on, Rose would be staying in the main house with her new husband. Her belongings would be brought later. The feast would last for three days; any less would be considered paltry. However, because they got married during a seasonal celebration, there was still a week to celebrate. They had the feast outside with all the eats and drinks. The honeymoon still awaited the newlyweds. Orinn had a surprise for Rose and sneaked away to meet with Popi in secret to hear if all was arranged.

Late evening, when it was time for them to consummate their union, two horses were brought forward. Everyone cheered, knowing what was about to happen next. Rose was confused about why they had horses. Orinn just smiled and said it was a surprise; she smiled broadly and submitted to her new husband.

When they rode past Popi's house and followed a path in the opposite direction, she knew where they were going and was extremely happy with the thought of being entirely alone.

Rose was nervous at first, thinking they would do the same thing as they did to Helga on her wedding night, where they took her and made her ready for bed before her husband could enter the room. She was relieved Orinn made other plans.

They arrived at the beach's deserted cottage; this was where it had all started for her. Her journey first started here with Popi when waking up with amnesia. This was her first home, and she was too scared to leave to meet the island's people at first, but now, everything has changed!

Orinn opened the door, picked Rose up, and carried her over the threshold. Once inside, she noticed someone had been here before, preparing the room for them. A fire was burning, and a lot of mead was placed on the floor. She laughed and remembered that the mead should last them a month, hence the 'Honeymoon.' If it ran out before the time, they believed there would be great displeasure from the gods and the powerful curse on their union. Rose remembered how she had worried for Olaf at his wedding, and thankfully he survived.

There was only one big bed in the room now where she remembered two small ones; the table and chairs were still there. Orinn sat on the bed cross-legged and asked her to join him, so she sat across facing him. Two candles were burning, and the light was just right, not too dark or too light.

Once they were both comfortable, Orinn asked, "Would you mind doing me a favor? I know we just got married, but would you forgo a true tradition of the ancient Viking ways of tying the knot, so to say? Binding our love for eternity."

"I would be honored to comply with my new husband." Rose smiled sweetly at those words and was very interested in this new activity.

He took a rag beside him and unwrapped it; inside was a small dagger and a long clean cloth that had embroidery on. On the other side was a small jar of ointment and two small bandages. Rose's eyes went wide, wondering what was coming next.

Orinn enlightened her, "I spoke to Popi about this, and she did most of the work. Don't worry; it's nothing bad. I will help you through this. They say if your love is deep enough and true, it won't hurt much." He picked up the dagger and cut a small slit in his open palm of his hand that had his wedding ring on. He held out his hand for Rose, and she offered her hand to him. The knife was sharp, she felt a quick nick, and it was over. He clasped their bleeding hands together and bound their hands with the embroidered cloth.

Orinn then looked into her eyes and said, "I bind our love for eternity - I will bleed for you, and I will die for you. May our love last in this life and in the afterlife. If I should pass before you, I shall wait for you until we meet again, for we shall. Our souls will forever be bound in love and sealed in blood. I take thee Rosaline to be my wife, and I shall never take another for you are my life."

Rose was not sure what to say, so she spoke from the heart, "I take thee, Orinn as my husband in this life and the next. My love for you will never perish; our love is eternal. I make this bond between us, and I swear in blood and bleed for you when I say, you are my life, and I shall always love you."

Orinn was surprised. He never knew she would be able to voice her true feelings. Even if she repeated his words, the bond would still be strong. Rose using her own words, he felt this was meant to be – they were indeed soulmates. He took the embroidery cloth off and rinsed her hand clean of the blood. Orinn rubbed some ointment on the wound and covered it with the bandage. Rose repeated the procedure on his gash. They got up, and he poured them each some mead to drink to their new love union, and before they kissed passionately, he said to her, and she repeated his words back,

"I belong to you. I am yours!"

"I belong to you. I am yours!"

They were still both dressed in their wedding outfits and wanted to feel more comfortable. Orinn took his shirt off – Rose was in awe of his build. She felt a little uncomfortable with this being her first time, and she had no idea what to do, but she badly wanted to please him. The best way was to follow his lead so she wouldn't humiliate herself.

Orinn stared at Rose; he wanted to undress her and take her in his arms and consummate their union, but he knew he had to be patient with her, and this would take some time – time he was going to enjoy. Rose was perfect and pure – untouched by any man. She was his rosebud – he wanted her to blossom with their love.

He kissed her hands and turned them over to kiss her palms, then went slowly up her arms to her neck, then her cheeks, and tasted her sweet breath once more. He was gentle and loving in his touch and kisses. He kissed her more on the neck, and she moved closer, then they slowly kissed again, gently at first, then it became more profound.

He pushed her slowly away and said, "Too fast, my little rosebud." He smiled. Still standing, Orinn turned Rose around and kissed her on the shoulders, and from behind, he slowly undressed her.

Her whole body was on fire by this time; Rose felt shy at first, being naked and allowed him to take charge. She wanted this to be perfect. She was intoxicated with his touch and kisses on her bare back. He traced his hands slowly down her sides, feeling her perfect curves. He slowly turned her to face him again, and he stared at her nude body. The way the candlelight was flickering across her milky skin – was too much for him.

Rose was beautiful and perfect. Her nipples were erect; all he wanted to do was taste all of her. Orinn held Rose close just to feel her nakedness against his chest and almost lost it. He led her to the bed, and she lay down; he still had his pants on and would keep them on until she was ready.

Orinn touched her shoulders, and once again, he traced his finger from her neck down to her hips past her privates, not touching her yet. He slowly worked his hands up to her breast and sucked each one, then started kissing her on her belly and up again.

Rose was moaning by this time; her body had taken control and moved with each kiss and touch. This went on for a long time until she thought she would explode. He decided it was time to undress, and Rose saw him fully naked for the first time. She was in awe of his full nakedness and became aroused. *Would they fit*, she wondered.

He laid down fully naked this time and drew her closer to him. Orinn started kissing her again; soon afterward, he went down to suck a nipple. At the same time, his hands went to her privates; he explored there for the first time and felt she was ready. Her moans became louder, and she felt a spark between her legs. He climbed on top, slowly entering, then stayed motionless inside and looked at her.

"Are you alright – does this hurt?"

Rose felt the pain slicing through her body and froze. She held on to him until the pain subsided.

"I'm fine. A little pain, but I'm fine." She smiled to reassure him. There was a slight sting, and then it was gone. He did not move; instead, he kissed her intensely until he felt her move. He continued to move slowly until she was used to him – they were both lost in their lovemaking. It was an effort to control his own release. When he felt her shudder, that's when he could breathe and let go.

They lay next to each other, panting, Rose in his arms with a broad smile on her face. They spoke for a while and made love once more before they both passed out.

Orinn was still sleeping when she awoke. It was still slightly dark outside, a new day beginning – she never slept that long. Rose got up and filled a plate with food that was there, took a jug of mead, and the food back to the bed. She touched his chest gently, kissed him on his stomach and chest, and watched. She waited for him to open his eyes – he smiled.

"You are going to be the death of me!"

"That's why I'm going to feed you first." She reached over for the bottle, and he had a big gulp, then passed it back to her, and she drank some as well. She sat on top of him while she fed them both. He watched her nakedness on top of him, and she was glowing. Her breasts were perfect and petite. Orinn wanted to sit up and kiss them, but she pushed him back down, and he chuckled. "What have I created?"

"You have awakened my body to endless pleasures and possibilities." She returned a naughty smile. Rose felt him awaken and laughed.

He grabbed her around the waist, threw her on the bed, and had his way with his new wife. They were happy on their deserted island and comfortable with each other by now. They swam at night and sometimes went for walks on the beach in the day but mainly stayed indoors. They dared to make love in the day on the beach and hoped that they weren't caught. It was easier to make love outside at night, and it happened often.

They were there for a few days until it was time to leave. Their food was running low, and the other mead that had to last them a month was waiting for them. They would be going back to the same house and sleeping in the same bed for the rest of their lives.

Rose had no clothes; only her undergarments were needed when they left the little cottage for walks. Other than that, they were primarily naked all the time. Dressed again in her wedding dress, they left their love haven. The world had ceased to exist, and now it was time to return to reality.

They stopped at Popi's, and she forced them to stay for lunch. Var came in to join them, which was unusual for him to do. He always ate his lunch outdoors in the fields. Popi could see this was a good match – Rose was blooming. Sigrid felt unsure of Rose's duties as a wife now and thought she might lose her friend. Rose surprised her when she asked what she missed out on with the herbs and asked Sigrid if she wanted to go for a ride early tomorrow before starting the day – it made her happy.

Rose still wanted her family close and would always need them. She did not want to feel that her marriage would change anything. She wants to explain this to Sigrid on their ride tomorrow. Rose still wanted to learn and come over during the day. The only difference now was that she had a husband to return home to every evening, and it was a good feeling. It made no sense why things should change. What must she do anyway if not come over and still work? She discussed this with Orinn, and he agreed. She had to be her own person. He never expected nor wanted Rose to change or feel the need to shadow him all day.

King Philippe had been on Orinn's mind for a while now. He was worried about his friend and the war he would have to face soon. He had no idea how to help him, and maybe if he spoke to his father, he might have some thoughts on the matter. Orinn needed to do something; he felt hopeless just sitting here while they were in peril.

They got home, and the villagers welcomed them back with more cheers, and Olaf came over to greet them. Orinn invited him in to sit with his father while he spoke of Philippe's predicament. Two sets of minds might be better than one, and Olaf was a war expert. After hearing about his war stories during their voyage, Orinn thought he might have more insights on the matter at hand.

Rose and Orinn went up to change first, then went in to meet the old chief. He was happy to see them and ordered drinks to be sent in. Kiti was there as always and was friendly towards her. They talked of some of the villagers and odd things while the men spoke, and later they were listening in. Rose was also worried that Philippe might lose his crown, and so soon after receiving it, he was a good man.

Orinn was saying, "If only he could marry well to unite armies and have extra men to fight, but who was the main question."

Olaf said, "That's not always the answer; your men have to be strong and willing to fight for the kings' course. One man should be able to handle at least three to four enemies."

"Not so easier said than done, my friend. Some of the men are afraid and not long in training or being in the war. Training needs to be given and motivation from someone they respect and will fight with. I was there – I saw them and trained them myself until situations changed, and I had to leave."

Rose could not help but to chip in. She had an excellent idea and hoped they would see it from her perspective, especially the old chief. She said one sentence and waited for a reaction from the men.

"We could unite our family with his?"

Orinn was the one that asked how.

"Well, in marriage, how else? Times are changing – look at us. Your men are strong enough to fight and are always willing and ready for any battle. Once united, we could ask the other tribes to join in." Everyone was silent.

"Who will he be betrothed to?" Orinn asked, not thinking clearly.

"Kiti, of course!"

"What?" Kiti stood up and was very upset with Rose for deciding her future for her.

"Kiti, listen to me before you storm out. That life over there is perfect for you. You're sad and lonely here, and there you will be envied by all and plenty of things happen during the day, you will always be busy with fun activities. The gowns you will wear and the balls you will attend, and Philippe is a great and honest man.

"You will be the Queen of France! How much better can you get than that? I just have this feeling that the two of you will get along just fine. Think about it. You will meet him first, see the place, meet the people, and decide before discussing it with Philippe. That is if your father and brother agree to this arrangement?"

Rose looked at them, and they said nothing. Kiti did listen, and it sounded interesting to see the place first and meet the people. She badly wanted to get off this island, but also did not want to leave her family. Still, Kiti wanted a life of her own. All she said before leaving the room was, "Maybe?"

Those words surprised the old chief, which made him consider the matter as well. His daughter needed a life and a good husband, but if this king was in a war, his child was unsafe, which meant they had to help him in a way. The chief words shocked them all.

"OK. There's one condition! I will go with and meet this man myself and see where we can help before any arrangements are made."

"What, father? You want to go with me? I don't think that's a good idea!"

"Why not? I am not sitting here and sending my only daughter out there where there is danger. I go, or she stays!"

Orinn looked at Olaf, "So much has happened now; I'm at a loss for words. How do you feel about fighting in a war one last time, and do you think the others are ready for this battle? I need to know how the people would feel about our decision first. I can't just send them into something they are not ready for."

"Chief Orinn, I am always ready and would love to fight one last battle before I retire and have kids. I think my Helga would agree, and she will follow. Have a meeting as soon as you can with everyone and hear their comments – we will go from there."

The following day, they had a village meeting where everyone attended, and most were not willing at first; however, close to the end, everyone was excited to fight for a good cause. Now Orinn was taking his father and sister to meet the King of France. A few weeks later, they were on the ship again. Orinn announced that Var was a counselor in the village while he was gone and in charge as his right-hand man.

13

Kiti felt energized for the first time in a very long time. She had never left her home before; this was an adventure that had her continually ecstatic. She was talkative and overexcited. Rose told her not to worry about clothing; she had a closet full of gowns and dresses. She explained, as soon as they arrive, the men would go in to announce their arrival while they took a bath and dressed to look presentable before meeting the king.

They docked at the exact location when they dropped Rose off a few months ago. It was secluded; traveling further to the main docks was time wasted, and they might run into unwanted ships. Their traveling time would be stretched as well; they wanted to avoid any unwanted or false alarms reaching the castle before they did. This side was closer traveling to the castle with not many houses around, mainly stretched out farms.

The old chief has not said much during their trip; he was unsure how this would all play out. Thankfully, he had his most formidable warriors with him if there were any problems. They would camp not far from the castle; only Olaf and Helga would accompany them inside. Rose knew how the people would react seeing the old chief for the first time; he was a huge man and very intimidating. She prayed that everything would go smoothly.

They approached the castle, Rose and Kiti went their separate way from the men. Rose ordered a bath before taking Kiti to her old room. Kiti has never seen this kind of life before, and her excitement turned to nerves. Now she felt like an outsider and felt guilty about how she treated Rose when arriving on her island for the first time. Kiti was amazed at the room and how big it was. She had no idea what outfit to choose. They were almost the same build, though Kiti was a little taller and had a full, healthy chest. When they brought the bath, Rose asked for someone to do their hair; they were busy for over an hour.

Eventually, they were dressed and ready to leave when Kiti said, "Rose, I just want to thank you for doing this for me even if I choose not to marry this man. Just being here and experiencing this new adventure means a lot to me. Moreover... I'm sorry about how I treated you before. It's just that I was jealous because you could leave the island and be free, and I was stuck there my whole life. I could not understand why you wanted to stay.

"Then it got more difficult after losing my brother to befriend you, and I'm sorry. Now, I feel how you must have felt around strangers and not knowing who you were or where you were. I was selfish – I'm sorry!"

Rose was stunned that Kiti had opened up to her, and she appreciated it more than she could imagine. They were sisters now, and Rose wanted to get to know her better. It was a start, and she was happy.

"Thank you, Kiti, that means a lot to me, and it's fine. I have your aunt to thank for making it easier for me. Now come, it's time to meet my king and later his brother Antoine, whom I think you are going to love."

When Orinn announced his arrival, Philippe was happy to hear his name again and ordered him in. He did not expect the company that followed and stood up.

"Ollie, my dear friend, you came back. What do I owe this pleasure to? And I see you brought company. I hope your reason for leaving us went well for you?"

"King Philippe, this might come as a shock, but before I introduce you and greet you, I need your blessing on my marriage with Rose. It would mean a lot to both of us that you are pleased with our union and bless it?" Orinn wanted this to be said first before anything else.

"Married to Rose!" he laughed, "Of course, my dear friend, you have my blessing. I knew something like this would happen. You are both good people, and I could not think of a better match than the two of you. And where is my lady friend? Has she joined you on your travels?"

"Thank you, my king, and yes, she will join us shortly. Now let me introduce you to my family. This is my father, the chief, you met Olaf, and this is his wife, Helga."

Philippe has never seen such a huge woman before; she was much taller than her husband and built larger in muscle than most men – and the chief! There were no words to describe him; when he entered, his significant presence dominated the room.

Philippe greeted them, "Olaf, my good man, good to see you again, and it's a pleasure, milady." He had no idea what to say to Helga and a lady she was not.

"Chief, I am honored to meet you, and a huge pleasure to be in your presence." The chief was still sizing Philippe up and had nothing to say; however, he knew he had to say something.

"Thank you!" was all the chief said.

Philippe was trying to hide his nerves. "OK..." His voice was the same as his build, big and loud. "We will have a feast tonight for you and your new wife and my new guests. Still, you have not said why you have come?"

"I have been thinking about your predicament, and I came to talk to you and see if we could help you in your war? My men are ready to fight and train your men if our meeting goes well."

"What meeting, you have me lost. I'm grateful for your help, but why would your people fight for me?"

"My father has stepped down as old chief, and now I am chief on my island. We come with a proposal to join our families if the two parties involved agree to it – to take my sister's hand in marriage. If both parties agree to the arrangement, my people will fight for you, and we can ask other tribes to join our fight. This will be *our* battle and not yours to face alone."

Philippe was taken aback by this proposal and sat down again, a loss for words. '*Marry his sister, and the Vikings will fight for him!* He surely needed the army, and the Vikings were fierce warriors, the kind of men he wanted – needed. '*His sister – who was she, and where is she?'*

"I don't know, Ollie, you have thrown a huge revelation at me now, and I have no idea how to reply. You of all people know I need the men, and my men need the training as well, but to offer your sister to me? It's a matter to ponder over. Let's relax and have our feast; then we can talk further about this tomorrow. My servants will escort you all to your rooms to rest or wash up, and we shall meet again in an hour in the dining lounge."

Kiti looked stunning, and not surprisingly, acted like a real lady; she walked tall, proud and radiant. They were both ready to meet the men and introduce Kiti to Philippe. Rose had a good feeling about this by just looking at Kiti. She announced their arrival, and they let her in. The men were gone, and Philippe was giving orders to a servant. He was expecting Rose to be alone, however, when he looked up, he saw Kiti for the first time, and he was speechless. She was the most stunning woman Philippe had ever seen, and his heart raced. He stood staring like an idiot, and she smiled. Kiti, too liked what she saw; they both stood staring at each other. Rose saw the exchange and was pleased.

"Good to see you again, King Philippe," Rose announced.

The spell broken with Roses' voice; he looked at Rose for the first time. Philippe walked towards her and said, "Rosaline, it's so good to see you again. And I see you brought a party with you this time around," he laughed, "You just missed them; they left a few minutes ago." He took her hands and kissed her on both cheeks and said, "And I hear congratulations are in order. I'm honestly happy for you both. Who is your friend?" He turned to face Kiti.

Rose laughed, "This is Kiti, princess of the Vikings. Kiti, meet King Philippe." Rose showed her earlier how to curtsy for the king, and she did it perfectly.

He bowed, took her hand, and kissed it. "It's a pleasure to meet you, Princess Kiti. May I escort you both to the lounge? I ordered a feast for my new guests and your union with Ollie, Rose." He never took his eyes of Kiti.

"Please, King Philippe, call me Kiti." She had no idea why Rose would call her a princess. However, she was feeling like one today, and it felt good.

"Then you shall call me, Philippe."

"Very well, I shall." Kiti smiled, and Philippe thought his heart would stop.

Rose was feeling uncomfortable and felt like a third wheel.

"Why don't the two of you go ahead while I go in search of my husband? I will meet up with you soon." She watched them walk away and saw all eyes were on them. Kiti was a beautiful woman, and Philippe was just as handsome. They made a perfect couple.

Rose could not wait to see Antoine again and went to his room to greet her friend. He was delighted and surprised to see her. She quickly informed him about the visitors and how the two acted when meeting. He was curious and interested in meeting her and the new company in the castle and said he would change first and meet her there.

Rose went looking for Ollie. She found him entering a room two doors away from hers. She knocked, and Helga opened it. The first thing Helga said was, "You should see our room!"

Rose chuckled, "Whose room is this?"

"The old chief," Helga informed her.

The old chief was out of his element. He kept looking around the room. When the chief saw Rose, he stood up and asked, "Where is my daughter, Kiti?" Expecting his daughter to be with her. Rose explained what happened, and the chief wanted to be there.

"We will leave now, father. She is safe with him and in this castle. You must please relax and try to enjoy yourself at dinner. Their food and drinks are different from ours. You might enjoy it."

They all walked together to the dining hall, and the people stepped aside for them to pass. It was a sight to behold; Rose was leading the way in front, looking like a real lady with the Vikings following from behind. They found Kiti and Philippe talking to other guests, and she was laughing. The old chief saw how transformed his daughter looked and was in awe to see this new side of her. She looked different and happy. When Kiti saw them, she walked over to greet them.

"You look stunning, my sister!" Orinn said.

"Thank you! I feel good."

"I agree with your brother; you look beautiful and not like my little girl anymore."

"Thank you, father. I like it here so far, and the people love me."

Thorarin wanted to know, "So does this mean you agree to this arrangement with the king then?"

"It's really too soon to ask, but I do like him. He is respected and seems like a kind person." Kiti did not want to be too forward with her feelings, but it had been love at first sight for her.

Orinn could see how Philippe was staring at Kiti and knew this was going to happen. Tomorrow will be a busy day for them all. They will be in meetings and making arrangements to build an army - and a wedding. Rose was right, this was the only way to help the king, and so far, it was working. Later that night, when Rose walked Kiti to her own room, Philippe called on Orinn to have a quick word,

"Ollie, I accept your offer of joining our family in marriage. I'm telling you this now so we can get straight to business tomorrow. I hope your sister feels the same, and I see your father has relaxed a little too. I would value his blessing before any of this goes forward. He seems like a powerful man, and I would like him on my side." They both laughed and shook hands. Before Orinn joined his wife in their room, he made a turn to his father.

"So, he agrees to marry Kiti?"

"Yes, he also said that he would like your blessing in this before it goes forward. It's now up to you, father? We will meet in his chambers to discuss the matter at hand, and if all parties agree, we will go forward with our men and send them to the camps."

Before Kiti entered her room, Rose told her where the others were if she wanted to see any of them. Kiti was glowing, and Rose could not help asking, "So... how did you enjoy your evening?"

"It was pleasant; I never thought it would be like this! I like it here."

"And...?" She laughed.

"And what?"

"You know! Do you like Philippe – will you marry him? They are going to ask you tomorrow, and trust me, he agrees to this arrangement full-heartedly."

"Really? I guess." Kiti smiled, and that was all she was sharing with Rose.

*D*uring their meeting, Philippe approached the old chief,

"I believe you have a score to settle with the English as well! I'm sorry for your loss, chief, and I do hope we can join our forces and win this battle."

Chief Thorarin had a restless night thinking about this arrangement. "You seem like a good man, though I don't know you very well, my son has high regards for you and is willing to fight for you whether I agree or not. To me, that says something about you, so I will give my blessings for you to marry my only daughter, but..." he paused and looked at his son, then back at Philippe, and said, "I have one more offer for you, and if you don't agree, then it's fine as well."

"Anything, my chief, name it!" Philippe was eager to please.

"I stay here in the castle too."

Orinn was shocked. "Father? You are not coming home with us when we leave?"

"No, if it's fine with Philippe, I will help him here if he will accept my help. I have run that island for too long! I have fought many battles and can give good solid advice on war tactics. My son, you are the new chief; that is your island now and your people. I trust and believe you will lead them well as I have. You and Rose together can handle any problems that you might face one day. I know that for a fact, you chose well for a partner."

Orinn had nothing to say, so Philippe spoke, "I will be honored to have you stay and receive advice from a wise man such as yourself." He looked at Orinn and asked, "Before we go on, may I ask that I ask your sister on my own time for her hand? I don't want her to find out from others or be told she has to do this. I would like a personal answer from her alone." Orinn understood, and he agreed.

"Now that that's settled, let's get down to business."

14

Rose and Kiti were invited to a picnic that Antoine organized. The two were getting on well, and that made Rose happy. However, she had no idea if Kiti should find out about his sex life or how she would react to it; she might be agreeable. Rose hoped she would, but for now, she mustn't find out. The picnic went well, and they retired early to have a rest before dinner.

Philippe fetched Kiti from her room to escort her down for dinner. He asked her about her day, and she said it was agreeable. Philippe asked again if she would accompany him tomorrow for a horse ride to show her the beautiful gardens around the castle. She agreed.

They met outside the stables. The horses were saddled and ready to go. Philippe took her to a beautiful place and asked if they could walk. He stopped Kiti at a fountain and took her hands.

"Kiti, I know we just met, and I must admit that when I first laid eyes on you, I knew you were the one for me. I have never in my life felt this strongly for any woman before; if I don't ask you today, I will lose my mind. I need to know if you feel the same for me as I do for you. The thought of you leaving again fills my heart with despair." He went down on one knee. "Kiti, will you please marry me and be my wife? I promise to be the husband you deserve, and I will make it my mission to see you happy for all our days together." He took out a beautiful ring that belonged to his mother and offered it to her.

Kiti smiled down at the beautiful man begging for her hand. It was so romantic, and his words touched her deeply. "Yes – I will marry you!"

Philippe slipped the ring on her finger as an engagement ring, stood up and kissed her full on the lips, which surprised her. She did not expect that so soon – she kissed him back. Her first kiss and it was electrifying.

They returned and shared the news with everyone. Orinn explained to her that their father would also be staying. He would not admit this to anyone, but he was a little disappointed. He just got his father back, only to lose him again. They still had this time together sorting out the army and strategy, and if ever he needed to see him, he knew where to find him in the future. When his age catches up with him, he feels that he would want to come home to rest on his island, and when the time comes, he would be buried beside his wife.

Philippe told Kiti that she could organize a ball to celebrate their engagement now that she has agreed to marry him. Whatever she wanted was hers. This pleased her, and her mind was already making plans. She would fit right in as queen, Rose thought. Kiti was not scared to give orders, this was her time, and she was in her element.

The training with Philippe's men went well. Olaf and Helga were in charge. The French army was not expecting a woman in the cavalry, but no one crossed her when she showed what she could do. Some even called her Sir. Chief Thorarin went there for a few days to motivate them, and it worked. The war lasted for many years, with many lives lost and battles won. King Philippe still had his crown and his queen by his side and knew he was blessed.

During that time, Kiti gave birth to a healthy boy; they named him Philippe II, and their second son was named after her late brother Thord. They had five kids in total, three boys and two girls.

Olaf and Helga had two boys, Askel and Baldr.

After the major war, when things had slightly calmed down, when Orinn and Rose were settled back on the island, she announced that she was pregnant and subsequently had healthy twin babies, Jacq and Ollie. Two years later, a girl followed – Sara, named after Rose's mother. Three years later, another girl came – Siv, named after Orinn's mother. They visited the castle often over the years and took Popi and her family for an adventure.

Popi had never left the island since first arriving with her sister all those years ago and was excited to see new things and the castle. As promised, Antoine was invited to one of the celebrations. He had a blast of a time and went as often as he could.

Sigrid got married to Tehran, the handsome and gorgeous son of the chief of the eastern tribe. The one who came to visit and spoke to them just after Rose was attacked while living with them in the beginning. Sigrid moved with her new husband and visited once a year before the last celebrations began with her new family. They would stay for at least one month before returning to their own island.

Rose was happy for her and took the role of being their next healer when Popi felt the need to retire.

When the time was right, Cnut married little Turunn, his shadow after her grandma died, Olaf's sisters' child.

After the war, Magdalene, Rose's handmaiden on the Viking Island during her amnesia, became close. Magdalene, as her wish, got her freedom and worked at the castle for a minimum wage. Because she had worked for Kiti's family all her life, she was trusted more and became Kiti's main handmaiden and was paid well. She married one of the stable boys and was very happy.

As predicted – Chief Thorarin came home when the age caught up and enjoyed his last days with his own kind and his many grandchildren. He lived a long and happy life to the age of 98.

Part three - last of the series, will be coming soon

A short story to enjoy and imagine what's next to come . . .

Introduction
Short Story
A few Years Later

"Sara Waters! Where are you off to again?" Rose called out to her eldest daughter. Her daughter was long gone and just waved her hand to her mother; while she rode off in haste on her horse, Rose stood there thinking for a while before going back inside.

They were all at Popi's place, having lunch. After they ate, they had to make ointments. Sara was not as keen on healing as her mother and Siv, her younger sister. Siv was fascinated with the art of healing, and she reminded Popi of her youngest daughter Sigrid, who was married and living with her own family on her husband's island. She missed her terribly, but Rose's daughter Siv made up for her loss.

Sara had more of Rose's open personality, wild at heart – it was uncanny. She had her mother's scarlet hair where Siv had a light auburn color, more of a gentle soul, not shy, but always polite and gentle in her ways. Both her daughters had her features and were growing up to be beautiful young girls.

Her firstborn, twin boys, Ollie and Jacq, she could not be prouder of. They were always helpful and loved being Vikings in a genuine sense. They took after their father in looks and build. Orinn was proud of all his kids; his sons were always with him when traveling.

Sara was the same age now as Rose was when she first arrived on the island. She was infatuated with Olaf's eldest son – Askel, a tall, handsome boy, a real Viking as looks go. These feelings started at an early age for her. They had always been close growing up together. Rose knew this and was pleased with the kids' affection towards each other. It was still too early to say if it was serious or not. What annoyed Rose was that her daughter Sara always found a way to run off whenever she had to help.

Cnut was always in the fields with his father, and his wife Turunn went to help her mother out on most days. She was nearing the end of her pregnancy, expecting their first child and still living with Popi. Popi felt that they should start thinking of building their own home. She did not mind them living with her and Var; it was just the two of them now and their many grandkids. But she wanted Turunn to feel relaxed in her own place to do what she pleased and change the area as she desired. Rose still came over every other day. She stayed away for a whole week once, not letting on what she was doing.

Popi never interfered with Rose's daily activities; if she did not want to share her goings-on, then it was OK. She was just grateful that she still had her eldest daughter Astrid and Rose; her two daughters were still close to her, and their kids were treasures. She loved them dearly.

Rose was busy with a surprise for Popi and Var, which she was not sharing until it was finished. Only then could she offer them the opportunity for a change and make that decision for themselves. When Rose came up with the idea, she had to discuss it with her husband first. When he agreed, Rose fell straight into the project and stayed away from Popi for a week to ensure they got her idea right.

She could not wait for that day to arrive, and it was taking its time. On most days, Rose helped with the project, and when the trade ship went out, she asked them to look for particular objects for her. Two ships went out now, one to France for training men and one on a trade but never at the same time.

Rose would ask Olaf when he was home on leave or asked Baldr, his younger son, to help build a few small necessary pieces of furniture and a lovely sizeable table from wood. She was thrilled with this new project, and the excitement grew more each day when it was almost complete.

Rose was about to turn to join Popi and Siv inside to help with making ointments when she saw Olaf riding toward her.

He looked worried, and she wondered what was wrong – was someone sick? Olaf jumped from his horse and landed with ease on his two feet.

"Rose – Rose!" Olaf called out, "I need to talk to you urgently!"

"What's wrong, Olaf – who's sick – is someone ill?" She feared there was another death on the island.

Olaf took her arm and pulled her further away from the house so they could not be overheard.

"No – no, Rose, something worse!"

"Oh my, who died?"

"No one yet!" He was angry.

So, it was a personal matter. Everyone was supposed to see her husband, the chief, with these things, but with Orinn's constant absence from the training camps, most villagers always seemed to approach her. Rose did not mind, but it was unusual, and it kept her busy anyway. Olaf moved out of the main house ages ago when his father passed and built more rooms for his family. He was pleased with his life and wondered what was upsetting him so much.

"Listen, Rose, what I'm about to tell you, you must please promise me that you will keep this to yourself until we get this sorted out?" He stared and waited for her reply.

"I promise! What's the matter?" She looked worried.

My son Baldr keeps disappearing at a specific time every day and comes home when it's late. When I ask where he was, he just says '*out*,' and that's it! I mean, how can I argue with him if I don't know what keeps him. That ain't an answer either, so I decided to follow him..."

"Oh boy! What did you find out?"

"Rose, please, I know I can trust you, so please keep this between us!"

"Yes, of course, Olaf - you know I will."

"OK, yes, I'm just... I don't know how to react to what I saw?"

"Go on with your story so I can hear what the problem is and see if I can help in any way."

"Yes, yes... um... Baldr was meeting a girl, and it would seem they are deep in it already because I caught them in action. They did not see me, so I left."

"Oh, so what's the problem?" Rose was a bit confused because that's normal for the young men to sow their seeds, so to say, before they settled down.

"It was a thrall girl - don't get me wrong - she's beautiful, and I understand why he's attracted to her, but it ain't a fling as you would think. This is serious between them! You can see that, and if this happens every day, then... I don't know what to think. That's why I came to you instead of Orinn. You do understand?"

"Yes, I see." She was thinking about this and asked, "Who is this girl?"

"Cutline."

"Oh, she's one of the new ones." They had a few willing servants that came from France that offered to work for them. They knew no cash was involved, but they got a roof over their heads, food and material to make their own clothes – they accepted this. France's main war has settled in a way, but there were still many battles that ensued. Their island was safe from any danger, and a person felt secure.

"What do I do about this? What happens if he's in love with her and wants to marry her? This will 'so' disappoint the chief, and I'm not talking about Orinn – you know the old chief still has his values, and this is a catastrophe!"

"Relax Olaf, let me think quickly." He gave her a minute of quietness and paced up and down. He was really worked up.

She came up with an idea – kind of. "Olaf, my dear friend, take all this away about her being a thrall and ask yourself, would you accept her then? Is it really a bad thing that is happening between them? Why don't you ask Baldr how he feels about Cutline, and then we can go from there?"

"Rose – I can't take everything away because what is – is! She is a thrall, and my son is a Viking! With you, it was different, you were a lady, and Kiti married a king. A thrall is a thrall. I know I must sound like I'm judging their differences in status, but I'm just trying to be reasonable. A fact is a fact! The village will be appalled by the news, and you know it! What do we do?" Olaf was anxious; He loved both his sons and was proud of them; he only wanted them to be happy.

Rose understood – it was almost the same as a gentleman wanting to marry a servant girl. That never happened, and it always just ends up as an affair between the two, but this was the same – she was not thinking straight.

"OK, I do understand what you are saying. Let me think this through tonight, and we can discuss this again tomorrow. Try to relax this evening, I think I will need to speak to him too, so I know how far this is, then we can take it from there. Don't worry; I won't say you followed and caught him. Just tell me where they were, and I shall go from there."

Olaf told her where he saw them and what they were doing. He tried his best to relax before going home; Helga would sense his distress, and she would not stop asking to know what was bothering him. He did not know what she would do to their youngest child if she found out.

"What do I say to him - why do you want to see him?" he asked while climbing back on his horse.

"Just say I told you to tell him to come and see me, nothing else. That's all I said to you."

"Right... Thank you, Rose. I will see you tomorrow just after lunch again."

Rose had no idea what to do. It was something that she had no say over, only the chief had. Should she tell her husband? Rose was thinking of Olaf and how close they were. He asked not to tell... She could not think - she was lost on this one. She hoped it's just a fling, and it would end when the infatuation was over.

Rose went home with Siv just before supper time to join her husband at the table. She still loved Orinn with all her heart, and whenever he and their two sons left to do battle in France, she would stress and cry herself to sleep on their departure and pray for their safe return.

Her project was almost complete, and she was close to calling for Var and Popi. Rose woke up early every morning to work on it before breakfast. When her daughters had their breakfast and were ready to leave, they would walk over to Popi's. Sara helped with other things, sewing clothes and preserving food. Orinn talked with her at times because she'd been getting a little cheeky lately.

She reminded Rose so much of Kiti and wondered if Sara should visit the castle to be rooted for a while. Sara loved her grandfather, the old chief; they were close. She might protest because of her affections for Askel, but he was there most of the time, though not as much in the castle. It might be good for both of them to be apart for a while. She would go with them in the beginning and let them decide whether they wanted to stay or not. Rose wanted nothing to be forced on them. Sara seemed restless and perhaps acting like a lady, and a few decent activities would change her some. Rose would have to discuss this with Orinn first.

Rose could never stop asking questions about the Viking ways – some nights, her mind was full of questions that burst out that her husband was glad to answer. When she could not stop, he always laughed and told her it was enough for one night and time to sleep. Tonight was one of those nights, and she only had two questions for him – they were getting less and less over the years.

When Orinn climbed into bed with his wife, he could see something was bothering her. He lay down and faced Rose, then asked with a smile on his face, "What's on your mind, my love? I can see you are frowning."

Rose smiled sweetly and said, "I have two questions that I'd like to ask you. It just occurred to me that I don't know how a Viking gets divorced – if ever they do, or is it allowed? In other cultures, I know you have to see a priest first and so on, but how do we, if we should?"

"Are you thinking of divorcing me?" He tried to look worried but laughed.

Rose gave him a stern look and was being serious when she said, "If you ever think like that, I'll have your head on a platter!" His smile disappeared, and she could not help but laugh aloud. "Please do tell me! This is really bothering me to know."

Like all her other questions – he thought. She had an inquisitive mind, and he loved her for that. "Well, my love, say you want to divorce me; you can only divorce me if I ill-treat you or the kids. Let me start from the beginning. Marriage; do you know that you don't belong to me?"

"What – I don't – why?" Rose was intrigued by this news. It was also upsetting because she belonged to him in her heart of hearts, and he belonged to her, no matter the new information and their different beliefs.

"Well, even if a woman gets married, she still belongs to her family; thus, you still belong to Popi and Var, as her daughters still do as well, which includes your kids at birth. You never

243

become a complete member of the husband's family – why? – I'm getting there." He laughed; her mouth was open and was about to ask why. Her husband knew her too well.

He continued to explain, "If her husband mistreated her or the children or was too lazy to run the farm well, she could divorce him. To get a divorce, she would have to call a couple of witnesses and proclaim to them that she was divorcing him. First, outside the threshold of their home and beside their bed where they sleep. Following this, the divorce was a fact."

"Oh, that sounds so straightforward and easy!"

Rose wanted to go on, but he went on speaking, "I'm not done, my love..." He smiled again, "It does sound easy, but there's still more to this. If the woman left her husband without good reason, the husband could keep her property and all her belongings, but if for a good reason, she would keep everything, and he would lose the lot! Meaning, the property, land, and if they have any kids, they will become custody of the mother – always, no matter the outcome. The kids are divided among the families according to the family's status. The children become legal members of the mother's family by birth and are protected by law. Women have more rights over their kids than men."

"Wow! So... If you become lazy and I do those things of divorcing you, I can kick you out of the house? Then everything belongs to me?"

"Yes, my love, everything!"

"Well, I must admit I haven't seen one lazy man yet on this island or a divorce, so this has never occurred to me to ask before."

"Then how did this question pop up in your head? Did something happen today?"

"No. After supper, it just came to me. I was thinking that I had never witnessed that amongst everything else that happens on this island. There's one more!"

"Fine, but then you will have to pay me for answering your questions." He started kissing her on her neck.

"And how is this payment going to go, in money or in favor?" She was giggling.

"Let's say favor!" Orinn kissed her full on the lips, and the kiss was intense.

Rose pulled away slowly, laughed, and said, "My question first."

"Go ahead; what's the next question?" He slowly started to undressed her while she was speaking. Rose was thinking about how to ask the next one carefully. She did know a little about thralls and their rights, thanks to Magdalene, her handmaiden when she first arrived.

"Has a Viking ever had relations or married or anything in that line with a thrall - slave - could it ever happen?"

Orinn thought nothing wrong with the question and continued to undress his wife.

He was kissing her naked body and stopped; while his hand slowly traced each delicate curve, he answered, "No - never; it was never done or even thought of. A slave was seen as property, the same as you would see or care for cattle. I know it sounds bad, but they do care."

245

Orinn stopped with what he was doing to think about how to explain this right.

"There are the non-caring Viking animals that would use any living women roughly to please their needs, but that was not true with all. If this were found out, the Viking man would be punished severely for his actions. The thralls were considered property and are seen as the lowest rung on the social ladder. They belonged to their masters, and if they had any kids, they too belonged to their master to keep or sell at an appropriate age.

"I must say that not one thrall can say that they were ill-treated on this island. It is said that immoral treatment of a thrall was looked down on by the owner. As such, they were all treated with care by most Vikings everywhere. A thrall's good behavior and hard work could earn them their freedom. They are always cared for through any illness or if being crippled through their services. So, 'no' to your answer; No one has ever married a slave or would consider the notion."

Orinn went on with what he was doing earlier. Rose set her mind's thoughts aside to please her husband.

Rose's mind was in turmoil the following day about Olaf's problem and how to handle it. While she was busy with her projects, she came up with an idea. She planned first to discuss this with Baldr, tell him that she knows about his affairs, and hear his feelings for this girl. However, if he knew she knew, then he might try to fight for his rights. Rose thought to take a different approach to this problem. She already told Olaf to tell

Baldr to see her; now she must think of a story to tell him. Baldr was good with his hands as his father and almost the same build, too, a younger version of Olaf.

A warship was returning soon, and a new crew would be leaving shortly thereafter. Her husband and sons were leaving this time – she might go with to settle Sara in, but that was another matter. She had to get her thoughts and ideas in order before speaking to anyone.

Rose's project was almost complete, and if she planned to leave on the next voyage, she had to get this done before then. She sent Siv over to Popi and stayed behind to try to finish the room she built and the one upstairs. Rose broke a wall down between two rooms to make it into one; she would leave it empty for now. She was excited and hoped this plan would work out too.

After having lunch, Rose was sitting on the bench in the gardens, lost in thought. She got a fright when Baldr approached out of the blue. He apologized, and she laughed it off then invited him to sit.

"My father said you wanted to see me, Aunt Rose." He could not think what the reason was.

"Yes, Baldr, I want to ask you something, but I don't know how you would feel about it. I will just ask, and we can go from there."

"OK..."

"Well, your brother Askel is always with your father when he joins the calvary and to the training camps, and I was wondering if you are ready to travel with them? You haven't left the island yet, and I wondered if you'd like to visit Kiti at the castle? Assist where you can and see what you can do to help around the castle. You don't have to fight if you do not feel ready, but it's good to see the world and see what's out there. I might be sending Sara as well and would like you to keep an eye on her, protect her in a sense." Rose was trying to make it sound like a favor and an important job. He would never guess her reasons.

"Please don't tell anyone that I'm thinking about sending Sara because I have not spoken to her or the chief yet. I don't know what her reaction would be."

"I won't tell, but can't Askel look after her when he's there? They seem very close, and she's constantly at the workshop when he's home, helping him out with odd jobs."

"Oh, really? I had no clue. I've noticed their attraction towards each other, and I know she disappears every afternoon, but not always to where. Thank you for telling me, but no, your brother is busy in the cavalry and is hardly at the castle, so he can't keep an eye on her. I'm asking you because I trust you will do the job of keeping Sara safe and out of trouble. Do me a favor, don't answer me now, think about it and discuss the issue with your parents, then we can go from there. I might attend in the beginning to settle her in, and if you go, I will help you find something to keep you busy. You are family of the king, so you are important when you are there. Think about it and let me know soon, please, so I can discuss this with my family."

"I will. Thank you, Aunt Rose."

Nothing more could be said, so she sent him on his way.

That done, Rose was rather pleased with the way she handled the problem and hoped it worked. She could not ask Baldr to be open about the girl he was seeing and would have to spy on them to see for herself. It was not in her nature to spy and felt uncomfortable with the whole idea, but Rose had to know without asking. After supper, Rose told her husband she wanted to work on her project to finish it, and he did not question her. She walked to the place where Olaf said they meet and hid well – and waited.

What Rose witnessed between the two said it all. They were in too deep, and if this came out, there would be big trouble. Baldr told Cutline what Rose said to him, and the girl was crying. Rose could not yet move from her hiding place and thought to wait for their secret meeting to be over. Rose felt awkward when they started to undress, and when they were distracted, she sneaked off quietly so she could not hear their cries of love.

Rose felt ashamed and guilty for what she had done and witnessed between the young couple. She hated herself trying to separate them, but it had to be done for his family's sake and their name. Baldr would be a disgrace to his family and the villagers. He would be cast out or worse, and she did not want Olaf and Helga to go through that pain.

Before Rose entered the main house, Olaf was waiting for her and asked where she was. Rose could not tell him the truth, so she fibbed and said she went for a walk to clear her mind to think. He thought nothing further and asked how it went with his son and what was said. Rose explained their conversation and told Olaf to leave it up to Baldr to confront them about leaving. If he refused to leave, the girl would be going in his place without his knowledge. It was cruel, but she was just trying to help.

The trade ship arrived, and Rose received her last items for her project and worked extra hard to finish it. A week later, the warship also returned, and a fresh crew would be leaving. She did not know when the warship would depart again and stressed about Baldr not returning to her with an answer. Rose would have to take a different approach and involve her husband if she heard nothing from him soon. She will have to speak to Orinn anyway to let him know what she asked Baldr and why she wanted to send Sara. Rose hoped he would agree, and they could both speak to their daughter. Orinn will wonder why it was essential to send Baldr, but she would shamefully repeat what she told the kid – whether he believed her or not.

Rose had never lied to her husband before, but she thought of her friend Olaf and what this would do to his family if the affair were known. She loved him dearly – he was like a big brother to her. He had always been friendly and caring towards her when she first arrived and kept her secrets to himself when she confided in him during his mother's funeral. He was a good man.

Rose told Orinn during supper that she needed to speak to him. She asked if he could see her while she was busy at the back on her project when he had the time.

When he finished his work, and before going to his room, he went to see if his wife was still busy. She was excited about her project, and he hoped Popi would like what Rose has done for her and Var – time would tell. Rose was still there, the place looked almost ready, and he liked what he saw. She had a good eye for aesthetics. Popi was going to love it!

"Hello, my love, this place looks complete!"

"Yes, I'm so excited! I will call them in a few days and talk to them; just a few small things still need doing."

"What's this you need to talk about?"

While Rose was still busy with small things around the place, she explained what she had in mind and her conversation with Baldr and sending Sara as well. Rose said she would go with her to settle Sara in and find something to keep Baldr busy.

"No," he answered when she was finished explaining.

Rose stopped with what she was doing and looked at her husband. "Why not?" Rose looked worried.

Orinn had no idea why Rose wanted to send Baldr away and still to protect Sara. The castle was full of guards, but he won't question her, though he did agree with Sara going. It would be good for her to see her Aunt Kiti again and her grandfather.

"What I meant to say, my love, is that you don't have to go. I will get our daughter settled and help find a position that works well for Baldr."

"Oh!" Rose was feeling relieved. "Do you mind speaking to Baldr about leaving?"

"Do his parents know?"

Rose tried to answer as honestly as she could. "I have asked Baldr to talk to his parents, but I'm still waiting for a reply." Rose hated lying to her husband and hoped this was the last time.

"OK, I will call them in tomorrow, now please stop working for tonight; tomorrow is another day, and come to bed with me." Rose smiled and followed her husband to their room.

After breakfast, Olaf, Helga and Baldr were called for a meeting with the chief. They were in his private study for a long time. Rose was anxious to know what was spoken. While they were busy discussing things, she went to her room and wrote a letter to Philippe, thinking he could help find a position for Baldr. She also wrote a letter to her dear friend Antoine, asking to help in this predicament, and shared her ideas. She hoped all went well in the meeting. She will pass the letters on to Orinn when he departs.

Straight after the meeting, Olaf searched for Rose and told her that Baldr would be going with them in a few days. It was settled, and he was happy. Olaf thanked Rose for everything she had done. Rose was relieved as well.

While walking to Popi's place later that day to have lunch, Baldr caught up with her to talk.

"Aunt Rose, will this be a permanent thing at the castle, or can I return on the next voyage?" He did not waste time on the subject. You could see he was upset with this decision that was forced on him.

Rose was speechless for a few seconds, and it never occurred to her to think that Cutline would still be here when he returns. She was an idiot! Her mind was racing again. How was she going to keep them apart?

"Baldr, we are not throwing you off the island, my dear. Of course, you may come back, but first, try to see if you like it there before you rush back. It's three full moons before you return; try to enjoy yourself."

"Thank you. Sorry, I did not get back to you, but I have had a lot on my mind lately."

"It's fine, love; you are too young to have any worries. Is there something that I can help you with?"

"No, it's fine, everything is settled - thank you!" He was off again.

Baldr was still young, and this must be his first love, which feels very powerful for a teen. She hoped with separation between the two that he might lose his infatuation with Cutline or meet another at the castle. From her own experience, she knew he would never forget her.

Rose's project was completed, and it was time to call on Popi and Var. She wanted to do this properly and before her husband left in two days. Rose wanted Orinn standing with her when she presented them with this offer. Everything was perfect and ready for them, and they were waiting for their arrival.

Popi wondered why they were called in; thus, they left straight after breakfast.

Rose asked them to sit down, and she started to explain with a huge smile on her face and was delighted to be able to offer this new change in their life, wanting them to feel comfortable. The only thing on Rose's mind was seeing them happy and would do anything to please these two beautiful people.

"First, I want to say that I know the two of you hope that Cnut can move out and build his own home with his growing family. Popi, I know you might have guessed that I was up to something for the many days I've been absent. I can eagerly tell you that I have a solution for both of you; I want you to listen first. I will show you, and please think about it before you answer."

"It's fine, my dear child, we will. Say what you want to say," Popi answered.

"OK..." Rose was nervous and excited. Orinn winked and gave her an encouraging smile, and she went on, "Please follow me, and I will explain when we get there."

They walked up to the first landing and followed her into an enormous empty room. Popi noticed a wall was broken down into an arch to divide the two rooms into one.

Rose turned to them and explained, "I would like to offer this room for the two of you. There's an area for the bedroom and an area for sitting, and you may decorate it the way you like. Bring whatever you feel you need. You can offer Cnut your home for his family to grow in. This is for you to settle in and relax when the years catch up with you. Var, you can still work in the fields and come home here from now on. It's just a proposal to think about – I'm not trying to tell you both what to do or give up your home if you don't want to! Please don't say anything yet. I don't think I'm selling this right to you."

Rose felt like she was losing and that it was a bad idea. How can she make this decision for them to give up their home for their son? Orinn kissed her and told her to continue.

Popi and Var were quiet; this was not what they expected.

Rose went on to say, feeling confident that the next room might do the trick, "OK, there's one more place I need to show you."

They followed, and she took them to a room not far from the kitchen. When they entered, Popi's eyes were huge.

Rose explained again, "This room is ours for potions and all that. It's not a kitchen, so nothing gets cooked in here, only our things. The fireplace is small enough for a quickfire and a basin with running water. Most of the things are here, which we need."

Rose gave time for Popi and Var to look around. All empty bottles were neatly packed on shelves and small pots, perfect for making potions or anything they needed. There was a huge table to work on, and four small round chairs were neatly set under the table, ready to be pulled out if needed. It wasn't a big room, but also not small. There was a curtain that Popi pulled aside and found two cots for injured or a sick person to lay on while they treated them. It was perfect – Popi loved it!

"My dear, *Lillé*, this room is perfect, but all my herbs and my garden are too far if we need things!"

"Oh – silly me!" Rose was so anxious that she forgot about the outside area. She opened another door that led them outside, there was a garden ready for planting, and there were already a few herbs budding.

"Everything is ready to plant whatever you need or want to plant."

"You did this all for me?" Popi was touched.

"Yes, I want the two of you to be happy and thought perhaps if you stayed here with your own personal room and our own workplace, it would be easier for you both, but don't answer now. We will leave you alone, and you know where to find us." They left before they could protest.

Orinn kissed her on the cheek and said, "You've done well, my love, and I'm very proud of you!"

Var looked around and said, "Well, my love – what do you think? You know Rose has our best interest at heart. She means well and thinking about it, that house is too big for just the two of us. You don't need to cook anymore and will have more time to relax and sew or make medication in this room. Rose put a lot of thought into this. The room upstairs is big enough for a lounge area to relax, and there's a nice balcony. I can easily go to the fields in the morning and help Cnut or help Olaf in his shop. We can get old here with no worries."

"So, you thought about this – you like the idea of moving in and living here? It's a lot to take in all at once, and she really has done a good job on everything – and I do love this room! We wanted Cnut to build his own place, so maybe if we give our home to him and move here, then all our problems are solved? Rose is truly a good girl, and I do love her with all my heart."

Var spoke next, "Our girl was thinking of everyone when she did this. She wants us all to be happy, and I, for one, like the idea. Rose put a lot of thought and hard work into this; I say we should do it. We don't need that big house anymore, and our kids are all grown up. Even if we stay there and Cnut builds his home, we are alone in that big house. She was thoughtful enough to give us a huge room for extra things. I can easily build whatever you want in the open space there."

With their minds made up, they went to tell Rose and thank her and Orinn. It took them the first day to discuss this with Cnut and his wife, and on the second day, they moved in, on the same day that Orinn and the others left.

It took them one day, with help from others, to move their bedroom items. Popi was still deciding what to take from the house. There wasn't anything she really needed, except the couch she constantly sat on to sew and the things she uses to make medications. Var was building them a small table and two chairs to sit on the balcony. He seemed more excited with this than Popi, but she, too, was happy. It was something to get used to. Var was always in charge of personal matters when the chief was gone; being inside the main house helped with this duty.

The men were gone for a month, and everything was going smoothly on the island. They would return in time before the next celebrations begin.

Having their workplace so close to the village helped a lot, and much was done with ease in the new room. Siv was happy that her moo-ma Popi and papa Var were living with them, and she too loved the new workplace her mother constructed. If people needed something, they came to the room and were helped immediately.

It was late one afternoon after supper, and Rose was still busy in the workplace. She still had Jessie's notebook of healing mixtures; she was trying a few out. Popi always looked through the book, too, and was intrigued by how some differed from hers. Popi was sorry they had never met; Jessie sounded like a beautiful person.

There was a knock on the door, and Rose called for the person to enter. She was busy stirring a mixture in one of the tiny new pots. In walked Cutline, and she was not feeling too well.

"Sorry to bother you, missus, but I thought to come to see if anyone was here. I'm not feeling too good."

"That's fine Cutline, what's the matter?" Rose took the pot off and let the liquid cool down.

"Not sure, missus, but I'm sick every morning, and my stomach is paining. I feel tired most days too. I thought it might go away, but it's getting worse! Though, the stomach pain is subsiding a little."

"OK, let me think. I can give you something for nausea and some pain medication; we can see how that goes. However, if it gets worse, I want you to come back." Rose looked at the girl and thought of something, "Cutline, are your breasts paining too? I mean, are they sensitive?"

"Yes, missus."

"Oh boy!" Rose sat down and looked pale.

"Is there something wrong with me – is it bad?"

Being straight with the girl, "You are pregnant!"

"Oh!" Cutline had not thought of that possibility.

Rose asked the girl, "What are you going to do?"

"Keep it!" Cutline looked confused with the question.

Rose would never suggest otherwise. "No, that was not what I meant. Who is the father?" Rose was going to be open with her and try to talk some sense into her. If Baldr did not care, then maybe she would. Not to sound cruel, but Rose should have sent her away rather than Baldr.

"I can't say, missus." Cutline looked down at her hands, feeling ashamed.

Rose stood up and pulled a seat out for the girl to sit and sat down herself again, then went on speaking, "Listen to me, Cutline. I'm going to be honest and open to you. First, I know! Second, do you love him?"

Cutline stared wide-eyed at Rose. "You know, missus – how?"

"Never mind how – do you love him?"

"I believe I do – I do have strong feelings for him," she answered.

"I'm going to explain something to you, and I want you to listen before you answer."

"Alright."

"How can I say this...? If this must come to light that Baldr is sleeping with you or even loves you, he will be disgraced by his family and not just him, but his whole family as well by the villagers. I mean the whole family like uncles, sisters, aunts and so on. You are new to this island and inexperienced with their ways, so you don't know anything about their culture. This for a Viking is really bad! I don't think you want him to be cast out or worse? I have no idea what they would do to him or you. I'm telling you this because I care, care what happens to him because his father is a dear friend of mine. His whole family will be looked down on with this affair. What upsets me is that he knows this and does not seem to care what he's doing, so I'm asking you to care for his part."

Cutline answered, "I don't know what to do? I do care what happens to him, but where do I go, and what would I say to him when he returns?"

Rose still had Jessie's cottage. Jacq, the young boy who had helped her then, still goes to the place once a week to see to it. He took the animals to his mother's home to look after them there. He said he would return them when someone moved back in. He gets paid well by Antoine once a month for his services. Rose did not know what to do about the place and wanted to keep it. It was waiting for someone to move in.

"I can help you with living arrangements for now until you are on your feet or decide what to do. The place is well away from any danger and is safe as far as I know. You can look after yourself by making cheese, candles, or whatever to sell to keep a living. After you had your baby and when you are settled, you can move on if you please. The place is yours for now."

"What about Baldr – should I tell him I am pregnant?"

"To be honest, I have no idea what to say to you. I will speak to him and hear what he has to say about his feelings for you, but I ask that you should try to stay away from him when he returns. It won't be easy, but try to convince him that you are too busy to see him. I don't want this coming out, for his sake and his family's. I hope you understand what I'm trying to tell you?"

"Yes, I do, missus. I don't wish him any harm, and his family is kind to me, but I must warn that he almost told on us so it could be out in the open. I said no to him, and he has to wait a while longer. So, it was a good thing then?"

"Yes, you were clever to say that. I guess we are going to have a problem when he returns. I can see it happening, and I fear for him. I don't want this for his family. Let me think for a few days, and I will call you. Go to bed and get some rest."

Rose could not sleep that night and woke up exhausted with worry. How should she handle this problem? What can she do? She should have confided in her husband; Orinn is an understanding person, but it was too late now, and she would not dare confess to anyone. She would try to handle it on her own. As the day went by, one of the sailors came and asked if she wanted or needed anything on their trade voyage again.

They were leaving soon. Rose said she would make a list and let them know before they went.

When the man left, it hit her; then Rose started to write a letter to Antoine and one to Jacq that was tending Jessie's house. She wrote a short one for Anthony, who lived in her parents' old home, asking if he could give a girl work if she arrived at his door and gave her name. Rose then called on Cutline to see her.

"Listen carefully to me, Cutline. I am trying to help, and I know you want no problems for Baldr, so I came up with an idea. You will be leaving on the next trade ship, and they will drop you off at a particular harbor. I will later explain the directions you will have to take to get to the house you will be staying in.

"Here are three letters; give them to a man named Jacq; he cares for the house where you will be living. Ask him to please deliver the others for me. There is one for him explaining your arrangements, for how long is up to you. I will give you some money to help you get by for a few weeks, and then you are on your own. There is a house not too far. When you feel you can't survive on your own, the owner will give you work. Does it sound alright to you?"

"That is more than anyone can ask for, milady. You have blessed me, and you are a very kind person to be doing this for me. It will be sad that I can't see Baldr again and him not knowing of his child."

"I do understand how you must be feeling and how he will feel when he knows you are gone. I do care, which is very hard

262

for me to do, too, not giving a child his father. I will tell him someday, though I think he will hate me when I do."

Cutline was thinking and asked, "Will milady do me one last favor?"

"Yes, anything, Cutline."

"Will you please help me write a letter to him? I will say the words, and you can write and give it to him, please. I don't want him to hate you or leave without saying goodbye. It might help him to get over me or understand why it won't work."

"That I can do."

Rose took her notepad and waited for the girl to speak.

My dearest Baldr,
As you will notice, I have left, and I ask that you do not search for me. Knowing you was the best thing that happened in my life, and I will never forget you. You will always be remembered, and I will always have a part of you with me.

You should look for another worthy of you and that can love you openly where I can't. Please don't be angry; this is for the best, and I hope you will see I was right one day and forgive me.

Cutline

Rose was teary after writing the letter and felt the pain Cutline must be going through – and what Baldr would feel when he finds out, but it was for the best. It still felt 'so' wrong, though. Thus, Rose made a promise to the girl.

"If he never gets over you and mourns for you, I will tell him where you are, and you both can go from there. However, if that does happen, I ask that you both keep this secret to yourself. The two of you can stay there and be happy together if it works that way, but you have to move on if not. Don't wait for him, though; he's still young, and he might move on. I don't want you to hope and have your heart broken again."

"I will, milady. I will try to send a letter if I stay on in the house or move on. I'm just glad there is work if I can't support myself on my own. You are very kind to me."

"I don't feel that I am kind and feel that this is all wrong, but I do wish you all the happiness you can find one day and soon a good husband that can love you and your baby as you both deserve." Rose hugged the girl and told her to return the day before the trade ship leaves to collect the letters and the money she promised to give.

After three months, the warship returned with her husband. Rose ran straight into his arms. When she looked around for her sons, she noticed one was missing and feared the worst. Only Ollie returned – she looked at her husband, and he reassured her he was safe and at the castle. He will explain later.

When they were settled, Rose ordered mead for them all. Olaf and Helga were there too, and it seemed they wanted to share something with her. Helga always went with her husband and still joined in the battles with the men. She was not the type of woman to settle down like the others. Her sons were grown up and were moving on. Rose also noticed that their son Askel had not returned as well?

"My wife, we have some news to share with you, and I hope you are pleased with our agreement. Askel came to me and asked for Sara's hand in marriage. I called her in, and we spoke at length about this. The two are very close. I called Olaf and Helga later to see if they agreed to the arrangement, and we agreed. A dowry was settled on that pleased both parties. I will explain later what was said. I want to hear from you if you agree to this before it's finalized and the wedding plans can move on?"

Rose was a little disappointed that she was not present for the discussion, but she was happy with the arrangement. Askel was a promising young man and came from a good family. Rose still had three kids where she could experience and discuss a dowry. She still had Baldr to confront and was not looking forward to that.

"I am pleased with the arrangement and happy for them," she answered back.

They had a toast to the family becoming united, and Olaf and Helga left. Rose had more questions to ask Orinn about the wedding.

"So, when is this happening, and when will they return? And where is my son Jacq - why has he not come back?"

"This might stress you out to hear, but you must know. Your daughter loves it there and might never return. When Askel found out she wanted to stay behind, he asked for her hand. The wedding will take place there at the castle in six months. We will all be on the next warship to attend the wedding. It is what your daughter wants, and I hope you are fine with it. You can see her whenever you please. Sara said she would return at times, but not soon and not to live here. I know it's sad, and you think you are losing a daughter, but she seems more grown-up there than she was here. I saw the difference and accepted her choice. Kiti and Philippe are happy to have her."

"Oh!" Rose was close to tears. "And my son?"

"Jacq and Ollie came to me and said they discussed it between them, and Ollie will be next in line to be chief. Jacq seems more at home in the cavalry and the castle as well. He will be coming home at times too. I think he has his eye on a young filly there. Decent girl, only time will tell."

"Oh!" That was all she could say. There was nothing to say about her kid's choices, and could have guessed this was bout to happen; at the time, she did not want to think about it.

"Are you fine with this, my love?" Orinn wanted her happy, not sad; however, he understood how she must be feeling.

"No, I'm fine. If they are happy, then I am happy! I'm a little sad; I'm going to miss having them around."

"I understand!" Orinn got up and held her. "The next warship will leave soon, and when they return, we will leave then. I asked that the warship return after two months, not three, so we can be there early in plenty of time if you want to help with the wedding plans."

"Thank you, my husband! I do appreciate that and would love to help Sara where I can."

Rose took a break after lunch to sit outside to think about everything and life, how things change and move on. How you think you know what might be best for your kids and they have a different point of view – not bad, but different. Rose was lost in thought that once again, Baldr startled her.

"How can I help you, Baldr? How was your time at the castle? I hope you enjoyed your travels."

"Yes, thank you, it was interesting to see new places. I am eager to be back home."

"Do you think you will go again?"

"I'm not sure. Maybe one day, I will see."

"I'm glad you enjoyed the outing."

"Aunt Rose, do you know the slave girl Cutline?"

"Yes, I do. She came to me when she was feeling a little sick, and I helped her?"

"What was wrong with her – do you know where she is? I hear she left?"

"Yes, dear, while I was treating her, she asked me if she could leave on the next trade ship, and I gave her some money. She's fine and well, just stomach pain. She left a letter for you if you'll be so kind as to wait while I fetch it." Rose was shaking while she fetched the letter. She couldn't believe how she lied to him.

When she gave Baldr the letter, he thanked her and was off to read it in private. Rose felt sorry for him and hoped he would get over Cutline somehow. Rose made a vow to herself to never lie again. It felt wrong, and she felt terrible doing it and keeping this secret to herself and not confiding in her husband. This was indeed the last time! She was a horrible person!

While waiting for the ship to return in the months that followed, the island ran as usual. When the warship returned a month earlier as Orinn commanded, the men who were going next to the camps and Rose would be joining her husband and son; they were all ready to leave for France. The ocean was smooth and peaceful on the voyage.

Rose was excited about the wedding plans and loved the dress her daughter had designed for herself. Sara looked happy and excited. Rose went to talk with Askel, and he promised to be a good husband and treat Sara well. Rose was pleased.

It was a huge wedding, and many people arrived to celebrate this occasion. Baldr was there too, and it would seem he liked a particular lady that attended. She went out of her way to get his attention, and he was pleased with his new companion.

While her daughter was on her honeymoon, and before the time came for them to leave, Rose wanted to visit Cutline to see how she was doing. She wrote a letter to Anthony and asked if she could spend a night there through her travels and that Antoine would be joining her. A letter returned saying it would be an honor to have them for the night.

When they arrived, they settled in the rooms Anthony provided, had a quick lunch that was offered, and was off again to Jessie's place. It has been roughly seven to eight months since Cutline left. She must be close to delivery time. Rose was happy to see the place again, and everything was the same. She still missed her dear friend terribly.

When Cutline heard horses, she came out of the little cottage and was surprised to see Rose.

"Good day, Lady Rosaline. It's good to see you again." For no apparent reason, Cutline blushed.

Just then, a young man came walking out of the house, and Rose recognized Jacq at once.

"Jacq, look how grown you are!" He, too, blushed. There was definitely something going on between the two.

"Good day, Lady Rose - good day, Lord Antoine. Good to see you both." They all greeted one another.

"Do you mind if I have a few private words with Cutline for a few minutes?"

"Yes, of course." Cutline invited her inside while the men had a chat outside.

"I thought I'd come to see how you are doing. I was worried and hoped you were fine."

"I'm fine, milady, thanks to you! Jacq has been around a lot and helping me around the house. He's a good and kind person."

"Yes, he is, and I'm very fond of him. So, is there something serious between the two of you that you'd like to share?" Rose smiled at the girl.

Cutline blushed again, "He asked me to marry him! He does not care that I am pregnant and accepts me the way I am. He wants to get married before the kid is born and said he would accept him as his own. I am so happy, milady!"

"I am pleased that two good people found each other. Please call him so I can speak to you both."

"I will now, milady, first tell me, how is Baldr? How did he take it when he found I was gone?"

"He was confused at first, and he hides his emotions well, so I can't say how he handled it, but he is fine now and seems to be moving on slowly."

"I'm glad to hear."

Cutline called Jacq in, and Antoine followed.

Rose spoke to them both, "I want to congratulate you both on your upcoming wedding, and for a wedding present, I am giving you this house. You can build on further if you please with extra rooms and so on."

They were both surprised and extremely thankful. Antoine gave his blessings too, and his wedding present to them both was a bag of coins. They were so happy they started laughing, and drinks were served to bless the union. They left for Anthony's place to have supper and rest before their voyage back to the castle.

Rose and Orinn were leaving soon to prepare for the coming celebrations. On the day they were departing, the newlyweds came out of their rooms for the first time to wish them a safe voyage back home.

Antoine asked if he could join them. He loved the way they celebrated for two weeks and brought Léo with this time to experience it.

When they arrived back on their island, while Antoine and Léo were settling into their rooms, Rose discussed a personal matter with Orinn. She felt it was needed. It was time to make that change and for him to come to a decision, to agree or disagree.

"I feel it's time to set the slaves free and not to accept any new willing ones that don't know our ways. Our island is growing, and there are plenty of hands to help out. The old ones that lived here have a choice, though." Rose thought of Magdalene's mother, who said she would not leave even if she had the choice. Those that knew their ways could stay, but the new ones would have to go. For her, it made sense. However, he was the chief, and it was up to him to decide.

"I hear what you are saying, and I will ask around if everyone agrees to this. I believe the older ones will stay, and that's enough help to go around. I also understand the new ones and see your concern. They don't understand our ways or accept them, and I had some complaints. I will think about this, but to be honest, I agree with you. It will be announced at the end of the festival. Those that should leave can leave with the warship, and those that are freed can decide to stay or leave."

Rose was relieved that he understood. She was happy to be back home and felt blessed to have all these people in her life. Soon she might have grandkids of her own. Siv was still content with her single state and did not want to settle down yet. Nothing was forced on her.

Antoine and Léo had a blast and stayed until the next warship left, which was not long after the festivals.

After everything was back to normal, Rose went to see her husband and asked him, "Do you know what day it is today?"

"I'm not sure what you mean, my love? It's a normal day, and I'm swamped." Orinn was teasing her and was busy with a surprise but would not say. He felt a little bad for seeing her sad but knew the surprise would make up for it.

Rose did not want to remind him and said it was nothing. She was a little disappointed.

Later that day, Orinn went looking for her and asked Rose to ride with him. He led the way. When Rose noticed the path that he was taking, she smiled. *He did remember!*

It was their anniversary, and they were spending the night in their special cottage on the private beach. Everything was set up for their special night. Orinn picked her up before entering the cabin, making her giggle, and then had his way with her. Later they ate and had a few drinks, and both were feeling a little tipsy; they went for a nude walk at night on the beach with no care in the world if they were caught.

Orinn thought his wife was the same as when he first laid eyes on her, and his love for her was stronger than ever. They were being playful on the beach and fell on the sand. He looked into his wife's eyes. "Rose..." He wanted to say, 'I love you, but the words would not come out. What he felt for her was stronger than love, and if there were another word for that, he would have said it.

Rose looked at her husband and waited for him to continue. When he did not, she smiled and said, "And I, you!"

They kissed passionately . . .

Novels by Michelle Walters

Three-part Series
Taken — Book one
Rosaline Labella Dumont — Book two

www.ingramcontent.com/pod-product-compliance
Lightning Source LLC
Chambersburg PA
CBHW052035240626
47153CB00006B/2096